Tales of Fates

Everyday Goddess
Stories
Volume 2

R.S. Kellogg

Tales of Fates

Everyday Goddess Stories

Volume 2

RKI

To Alicia

Introduction

Fate.

Such a powerful word, and a concept that has a lot that we can unpack.

In mythology, the Fates are three sisters who according to some myths live together in a cave, endlessly spinning, measuring, and snipping the threads of all lives.

Some say the Fates have power even over the gods.

In everyday usage, fate can be used to talk about anything from a destined and charmed romance, to a seemingly inevitable course of action that someone might be resigned to but not thrilled to fulfill, to a story or character's end.

Isn't it interesting how the word fate—the concept of fate—can play with the concept of choice, of spinning something new with what someone has been given?

If fate is in the ruts of lives lived unexamined, the patterns that are walked through as if they have always been there or must definitely be there, and choice represents a moment where a character wakes up to the option of new possibilities, it becomes very interesting to see how these two threads can weave together:

The unexamined, seemingly predetermined, odds-are-that-what's-going-to-happen-is-already-set-in-stone domain of the gray masses of fate can sometimes meet life-giving moments where something unexpected has the opportunity to happen. Where change is real, and all bets are off.

Maybe the great illuminating moments of opportunity that come up, though, could themselves be called fate—that is if the character chooses to take them (in which case we're back in the realm of choice again).

Or perhaps this pairing of fate and choice is a profound romance between to opposite concepts with tension between them. (Maybe they have a romance of fate.)

I've pondered before that for a story or a life to have cohesion but also meaning and power, they need a combination of the stability of the expected and the moments where the unexpected can break through. Presence is a good concept to pair with this, I think. The more present I can be to writing a story, the more I can sense where illumination and the unexpected want to come through. The more present I can be to my own life, the more I see possibilities within each moment and can make more conscious choices.

When I was an avid devourer of myths and stories as a schoolchild, I was delighted by the power and domain of the gods and elementals, and the way that their actions had a dramatic impact on the stories at play. So much could result from a single choice or a chance encounter. So many stories could rise up from the interplay of relationships.

As I got older, I learned how the ripple effects of a story could shape not just how a civilization explained things to itself, but also how it chose to focus its attention and what it chose to value. The characters that we told stories about carried weight, as did the stories we chose to tell. I began to become interested in stories that explored and gave meaning to the nuances of relationship, and to what people held most dear (sometimes things that are very unexpected). My ears perked up when I read or heard stories that spoke to my heart, stories which spoke to what creates themes and resonance in an individual life.

Stories can help us explore and build meaning, but at their heart I enjoy them as a form of play, a space where imaginative exploration questions can be asked, such as:

What happens next?

What would happen if this other thing happened?

And what more could there be to the stories of particular characters than what we may have originally seen?

What are the characters up to whose motives and actions we may not always see?

This volume of Everyday Goddess Stories follows goddesses and women interacting with Choice and with Fate. This book also has stories about the Fates themselves.

In "Nike Plays Cards," the goddess of victory shows up for her regularly scheduled card game with the gods planning on an easy win. Will she get more than she bargained for?

In "Fates' Colored Water," the Fates prepare for a birthday celebration for Atty. She's the one who snips the threads of lives and she definitely needs a day off.

In "Her Great Lengths," Rapunzel gets a rare opportunity to make an unusual choice in her normally tightly proscribed tower life. (Maybe it's fate.)

In "The Quilt of the Fates," Lach gets a headache when she looks deeply into one of the life threads she must measure.

In "The Women's House," a story set in the Breadcove Bay story world, a woman chooses to seek help to move through the weight of her grief.

In "Nike and the Fates," the goddess of victory visits the Fates to ask for a favor.

"A Cold Mermaid Tale," the bonus story at the end of the book, is the first story from my Mermaid Magic Tales collection and will give you a taste of that series.

A note on names:

In classic Greek mythology, the names of the three sisters who craft the threads of life are Clotho (Spinner), Lachesis (Allotter), and Atropos (Inflexible, the one who cuts the threads). In my collection, the Fates have given each other nicknames to go by, the way I and my sisters have done. Here, the Fates are Chloe, Lach, and Atty.

I like the idea of the Fates mirroring in their own way the kind of crafting that women have done for generations when they've gathered together. As a descendent of crafters and quilters, myself, it's easy for me to imagine Chloe, Lach, and Atty gathering to spin and manage life threads the way I've seen women gather to quilt and craft and talk as they tend to things that will serve their own lives and those of their families and loved ones.

The lives that they themselves work to help care for and tend.

Enjoy the stories.

Cheers,
R.S. Kellogg

Table of Contents

Bonus Story:

R.S. KELLOGG

AN
EVERYDAY
GODDESS
STORY

NIKE
PLAYS
CARDS

Who will win the card game of the gods?

Nike Plays Cards

by R.S. Kellogg

It's fun to be a goddess of victory.

Until you need opponents for a game of cards.

Nike, goddess of victory, sat motionless at her place at the card game of the gods, seated at a rickety card table.

This still being a card table of the gods, "rickety" by the divine definition was still beautiful. The cold surface where she drummed her fingers impatiently was inlaid with a glistening mother-of-pearl panel that had a few dull spots where it had been worn down by repetitive placement of holy elbows. A charred spot on the corner where a lightning bolt had glanced off the side of the table gave a silent clue as to which leg was rickety below, and also served as a silent reminder that the gods best behave themselves if they wanted to keep their card game friendly.

The card table had been in the family for centuries—it was the original card table, in fact, and had served as the divine blueprint for all earthly card tables, which may also have explained why so many of humanity's card tables were also rickety.

At this point, the gods' attachment to the table may have been more sentimental than anything else.

It was the card game they had always used for their friendly card games.

They had never used a different table.

So, they continued to use it, even with the scorch mark and the rickety leg.

The air smelled of butter, glaze, and cinnamon from the hot, fresh cinnamon buns sitting on an ornamental green glass plate on the corner of the table. Nike didn't have much of an appetite for desserts, so she pushed the plate slightly toward Zeus, who had already eaten two.

The slightly unstable table rocked just a bit under the weight of the shifting plate, and Zeus grinned at her, a couple of cinnamon bun crumbs in his beard. He jovially helped himself to a third.

She suspected that Zeus had ordered the cinnamon rolls as treats for the table with the knowledge that both Nike and Hera—the two goddesses who were present—would turn them down, leaving more for him.

But she overlooked the selfishness for now.

She had bigger fish to fry.

Nike was a more minor goddess, and only invited to a card game of the gods every few weeks or so.

The winner of the card game got to ask a favor of Zeus, unless they annoyed him too much.

And Nike had something she wanted today.

She wanted to upgrade her victory torch to something sleeker and more modern. Something beautiful that befitted her as both an ancient and a modern goddess.

To make the switch on an official level, she needed approval from the highest level.

Which meant playing nice with the king of the gods.

She glanced at the empty chair to her left. All they were waiting for was one last player. Hermes wasn't scheduled to play, but hadn't put in an appearance.

She wondered idly what might happen if Zeus ever won a card game, but that had never happened, so far as Nike knew. If anything, she thought, perhaps Zeus used the card games to doll out favors to the other gods in an organized way. If you wanted to take a petition to Zeus, you just needed to wait for your turn at the table. And then, your odds were pretty good: one out of three of the players facing Zeus would turn up as a winner.

And of course, when Nike was at the table, the winner was almost always her.

True, there had been a few times in which she hadn't won, and this was enough to give her an edge of nerves, because she really wanted to win this one.

But she was hopeful, and as confident as she typically was.

Nike sat at a folding chair which had padding on its seat far more comfortable than any folding chair had a right to be on earth, silently displeased at the fact that the back of the chair pressed against her in a more uncomfortable way than any folding chair had a right to do.

It probably didn't help that Nike had wings which she needed to tuck behind her when she sat down, and therefore preferred chairs with more padding or a more thoughtful design, but still.

Given that the table was owned by Zeus, she figured maybe having chairs with uncomfortable backs was deliberate on his part—can't let other players be getting too comfortable during a card game of course. They needed to get up and go after the game, not linger and talk his ear off.

Or, baring this, perhaps the powerful king of the gods had not yet figured out how to make chairs more comfortable—suitable for a goddess. It could have been one of those unnecessarily tough machismo things that Nike tended to roll her eyes at.

Or maybe, she mused darkly, the other chairs at the table might be fine, and maybe Zeus always gave her an uncomfortable chair on purpose—to try and keep the goddess of victory on edge, and thus somewhat more likely to lose.

As if.

The marble floor where Nike now tapped her impatient sandals was polished to a high sheen, and harp music from a muse drifted over from just far enough away to reassure the players at the table that their conversation was probably out of anyone else's divine earshot.

Flasks of mead sat at the table for the gods' pleasure— although Nike preferred the green smoothie which she'd brought for herself in the tall, thin reusable thermos in front of her, which she sipped at with a long fat straw.

She rested her chin on her fist, and sighed.

Zeus was chewing up the last of his most recent cinnamon roll, and Hera sat directly across from her, hands folded and calm. But the seat to Nike's left was, suspiciously, still empty.

"So why isn't he here already?" she asked.

Zeus glanced awkwardly at Hera, whose long brown hair was piled up on top of her head behind her circlet crown.

Both Hera and Zeus shrugged.

Nike glowered. "He's afraid to play with me after last time, isn't he?"

Hera smiled warily, her gray eyes seeming to see both the present and the beyond. "He said he'd be here," she said. "Maybe he's just running late."

Raising her eyes toward the azure blue sky overhead, Nike pouted. "I can't help it if I'm the goddess of victory," she continued. "Some gods just need to try harder."

"Relax." Zeus had one foot propped across his other leg, making a triangle with his knee. He was shuffling the deck of cards in front of him on the table. The cards made a perfectly paced cascading paper sound as they came together flawlessly, as he shuffled them over and over again. These cards had been a gift to the gods from a previously unknown but now rather famous artist down on the lands below. His gift to the gods had gotten him all manner of divine assistance in advancing his career. The cards of the decks featured gods and heroes of various realms, and Nike found all of the art luscious and fascinating.

She especially appreciated that her own image appeared in the deck—in the card of Victory, Nike looked snappy, with her wings spread at an attractive angle, and the wreath of victory spinning around one of her fingers.

In the image, she wore a pair of blue-rimmed sunglasses. After she'd seen her portrait depicted this way on the card, she had immediately liked the look of it so much she'd obtained her own pair of blue sunglasses in that style. She had to admit, they had panache.

Nike felt smug every time that card ended up in her hand.

She was already planning to approach this artist about coming up with a design for her new, modern torch.

Playing with the cards almost absently, Zeus laid a few of the cards down on the table.

"I think he isn't going to come," Zeus announced.

"What?" said Nike. "Oh." She looked down at his spread, and saw that Zeus had made his own divinatory layout with the card deck of the gods.

Hermes (the first card) faced a sea monster (the second card) while in pursuit of a nymph (the third card).

"He looks a little distracted," Zeus said.

"Not that you'd have any sympathy for his current quest," Hera quipped, and Zeus gave her a hurt expression.

"Maybe we should cancel today's game," said Zeus.

"No!" said Nike, and the other two looked at her, startled. "Well, I only get a turn at the card game every so often," Nike said. "Who are we going to invite up to finish the circle?"

Scooping up the cards again, Zeus shuffled them together, and rapidly began laying them out.

All of the cards which he was flipping over were coming out inverted: upside down gods, goddesses, heroes, monsters, and elementals.

"Busy, busy, busy, busy," Zeus muttered as he flipped through them.

"They can't all be refusing to play," Nike said, annoyed. "That's hardly sportsmanlike."

21

"Do you have any recent petitioners?" Zeus inquired, looking up at Nike with a piercing stare. "Perhaps one of them may come up and fill in the last spot for the chance of an audience."

"Fine," Nike said grumpily.

She stood, and paced a short distance away.

The other gods and goddesses tended to have many temples and holy places—and some of them had a plethora of places petitioners could come with questions or requests.

Nike didn't like to bother with all of that formality. In general, she sub-let space in the holy spaces of Zeus and Athena.

She felt this was a cunning and efficient arrangement: Whenever a petitioner came to one of those spaces, they invariably petitioned Zeus or Athena first, and threw on an additional petition to Nike after that—if they spoke to her at all. After all, Zeus and Athena were two of the main gods. And therefore, in the minds of most petitioners, far more likely to be able to come up with satisfactory results for a request.

Nike hadn't really been in high demand in day-to-day life since her statue had been removed from the Roman Senate centuries earlier. Before that, she had enjoyed a fairly active life supporting politics.

These days, prayers sometimes flew up to Nike from athletes, just before a race, or from today's politicians, also just before the results of a race (of a different sort), but these were such a fast matter that there wasn't really time to call one of them up to sit in a card game to determine an outcome. The prayers were typically like fish flipping out of a stream long enough for her to bless them before they sank again beneath the water. Sometimes one of her favorites with better foresight petitioned her more in advance, giving her time to personally petition the Fates on their behalf. But all she could see today were the last-minute prayers. Pulling one of those sorts up mid-prayer would merely subvert their flow, might undermine them, and would be hardly sportsmanlike on her part.

However, there was one small temple which some enterprising folk had put together to honor Nike and which was still in operation.

It was a small affair.

A pilgrim had to be very *dedicated* to find that one.

But it was this small, personal temple to which Nike looked now.

In the holy alcove of Nike's temple, she saw a man petitioning a statue of her in the space below.

The man had a seriously furrowed brow, and he had hands in prayer, with his head tipped forward to them, muttering rapidly but still—so far as Nike could detect—he was a sane person.

"You'll have to do," she said. "You're my only current supplicant who's taking long enough in prayer for me to currently have a conversation with."

And just like that, the mists of the temple came up, and the man stumbled, and was knocked into the Other Realm . . .

. . . Where Nike caught his elbow in the middle of his stumble.

"You'll have to look out for the card table," she said. "It's rickety."

"Oh?" said the man, in smooth tones, and Nike looked at him more sharply.

"Who are you?" she asked him.

"I'm Dave," he replied. Dave smiled crookedly. He had a chipped tooth, and wore sensible outdoor clothing—jeans, hiking boots, and a t-shirt that said "All Sunsets are Created Equal." On his head he wore a sunhat, and on his chin he had about two weeks' worth of beard growth. He carried a hiking backpack on his back, and he smelled like a tourist. A sweaty tourist. "You Nike?" he asked.

Feeling annoyed at Dave's pronounced lack of respect for being in the realm of gods, Nike nodded curtly.

"Cool," said Dave. "Pleasure to meet you!" Dave had something like a midwestern United States accent, but Nike felt that she couldn't quite place it. "Pardon my manners," said Dave, and he removed the sunhat, which he rolled up compactly and tucked into his back pocket. "I heard from my granny that a man isn't supposed to keep a hat on in church. Seeing a goddess is kind of like church, right? Only better?"

Nike nodded grudgingly, charmed a little despite herself. "You were praying a minute ago," she said. "What's your petition, Dave?"

"Oh!" Dave perked up. "Nothing like getting to speak to the boss herself."

She folded her arms.

"My buddies and me, we've made a plan to climb some of the grandest peaks in the world, right?" he grinned crookedly. "I've come to ask you for your favor, seeing as how we can use all the luck we can get."

Nike refrained from the impulse to rub at her eyes from this massive luck request. "I presume you've trained for this kind of thing?" she asked.

He nodded seriously. "We all have," he said. "Hiking isn't my main thing or anything, but I've been putting my prep work in. And I promised my wife I'd petition the gods for support before we all go. She's spiritual, that sort of thing, you know?"

Nike raised her eyebrows and nodded, imagining what the conversation would be like between Dave and his wife when he went home.

"Well, I have a deal for you, Dave," Nike said. "Here's my offer. We're playing a friendly card game of the gods. We need a fourth player. You play with us and you win, I'll throw some good blessings toward your goals. Play with us and you lose, no promises."

Dave shuffled his feet a little. "Card game with the gods, you say?" he asked. "Who else is playing?'

The king of the gods raised his hands. "Name's Zeus," he said, and nodded agreeably.

Dave respectfully bowed. "Pleased to make your acquaintance your majesty," he said, and Zeus chortled quietly.

"I'm Hera," said the queen of the gods, and Dave looked at her hard before bowing to her in turn.

"It's an honor," said Dave. He looked down at his hands and counted on his fingers. "So. The king of the gods. The queen of the gods. And my lady victory." He narrowed his eyes.

"Is something wrong?" asked Nike.

"Well, it's just that typically in the myths I've heard of, if someone fails in a challenge of the gods, bad things will happen," Dave said. "So I feel compelled to ask you here, is there any level of additional downside to this game, aside from me not getting good luck for my hiking?"

"You may get bad luck for the hiking if you don't play," Nike said. "If you need more challenges than that I'm sure we can be creative."

Dave startled. "Well all right then," he said, and headed for the fourth seat at the table. He set his heavy backpack down on the ground beside him. His chair made a faint scraping sound against the marble as he pulled it back, and then it creaked slightly under his weight as he settled into it. "Say, this is a really comfortable chair," he exclaimed.

Nike nodded, watching, and when he leaned against the back of the seat, and then he winced and sat forward again, she grinned to herself.

"Take a seat, Nike," Zeus said. "And let's play."

Nike took her seat and offered Dave one of the hot cinnamon rolls. A nymph came by and offered him a flask of mead, which Nike could smell the aroma of honey from.

"Man, this is awfully rich food," Dave said but that didn't stop him from eating an entire heavenly cinnamon roll in about ten seconds. "Have to watch my diet with all this upcoming hiking," he told Nike as he took a tiny sip of the mead. And then a longer sip. "Of course, I can't pass up the hospitality of the gods, now can I?" Dave gave a satisfied sigh.

Nike wasn't certain if Dave struck her as the kind of man who had the discipline to hike the major peaks of the world.

Also, she'd noticed while he was eating his cinnamon roll that he had a little bit of dirt under his fingernails. She wasn't sure what his level of attention to detail might be.

"If you're quite ready, we can start," Nike said.

"Go ahead," said Dave.

Zeus dealt the first hand.

When Dave picked up his cards, he exclaimed over the beautiful artwork. "Is that you?" he asked, showing a card of Hera to all of them. "Why it's beautiful!"

Hera smiled, accepting the compliment and inclining her head.

"Don't show us the cards," Nike told him sharply. "Now we have to re-deal."

"No re-deals," Zeus said grumpily. "Otherwise we're meddling with Fate."

"But we all know one of the cards he has! It isn't fair!" insisted Nike.

"We don't meddle with the *Fates*," Zeus boomed. The bag holding his lightning bolts, which was fastened to the back of his chair vibrated slightly, and Nike startled in her seat.

"All right, if you feel that strongly about it," she said.

"Not good to mess with fate, that's for certain," Dave said. "This king is wise."

Nike rolled her eyes and Zeus gave a brief smile.

The rules of the card games of the gods are complex. Nike hoped that Dave would get confused by them, and maybe play like a fool and lose outright.

But unfortunately for her, he turned out to have quite a good hand for the first round.

"So my last card is a satyr," said Dave, flipping it from his fingers so it somersaulted in the air and landed on the pile of the cards from the round. "If I understand the game right, that means I take this one, correct?"

Oh shoot. Nike's eyes were huge as she looked at the satyr that had won Dave the round.

The cheeky little beast on the card was depicted as making a rude gesture in the artwork.

At the moment, it was tough for Nike not to take it personally.

Zeus patted her arm. "Cheer up, Nike, there's two more rounds to go."

She nodded. "Beginner's luck," she told Dave. "Let's see what you've got for the second round," she challenged him.

He nodded. "Bring it on, if that's an appropriate thing to say to a goddess."

"I'll give you leeway under these circumstances," she said.

"Got any more of them cinnamon rolls?"

There were two cinnamon rolls left, and Nike was feeling defensive.

"No," she said. "Besides, you don't want to get fat for your hiking."

"C'mon," said Dave. "You can't tell me you're going to eat them."

Nike defensively picked up a whole roll and shoved it into her mouth. She washed it down with her green smoothie, staring at Dave in a challenging way the entire time.

"That combination looks disgusting," said Zeus.

"Well, I guess between those two items, it balances out to be healthy," said Hera.

"Your green smoothie smells even better than my drink," said Dave. "It smells healthy."

"Hmph," said Nike, folding her arms but again feeling slightly mollified.

Zeus dealt out the second hand.

For this one, Nike had a really good hand. She had Zeus himself! And also Hades, and Poseidon. Big three in the hand, she could pretty much take the round.

Only this time . . .

"Well, what do you know?" Zeus chortled after he'd played first one, then a second, and then the third fate to counter Hades, and Poseidon, and then Zeus himself.

Nike's face fell. All three of her big power cards had fallen to what had been essentially Zeus's wildcards.

"I told you, Nike," Zeus said, scooping up the cards to take the round. "No god can cross the Fates."

"You never win," Nike said, shaking her head in disbelief.

"Well, I just did! And you don't have to call attention to my poor track record," Zeus said, sounding hurt.

"Interesting positioning," Hera said. "If either of the men take the next round, they'll win. But if either of us takes it, we'll be going longer."

"Then one of us had better take it," Nike said, leaning forward, focused on the deck with determination.

Her hand this time was a mixed bag: she had Persephone, but also Apollo and Demeter. This was a weird combination, and there was no easy way to play it.

She watched the other players carefully.

Zeus was absently nibbling on the last cinnamon roll. The focused gaze to his face told her that he found his cards very interesting: probably a decent hand.

Hera looked bored.

But then Hera always looked bored during these games. She probably mainly came for the gossip.

Dave . . . looked sweaty. Little bits of sweat were beading on his forehead, and he was smelling more than he had before. Maybe like he already was the hiker he claimed to want to be—after said hiker had gone a few miles in the sun.

"What is wrong with you?" Nike said. "Are you nervous?"

He nodded his head. "Heart rate is up," he said. "May have just hit me that I'm actually playing a round with the gods."

She snorted and shook her head. "Finish the game, and after that it can all seem like a dream."

Blinking at her, Dave nodded. He looked a little faint.

"Maybe the cinnamon roll had too much sugar for his system," Hera said.

"I'm fine," Dave said, and took a slurp of Nike's green smoothie.

"Hey!" Nike said, too appalled to snatch it back.

"Feeling much better now," Dave said, sounding slightly stronger. "I think the mead was too much for me."

"Well, you are a mortal, and not a god," Zeus said indulgently. He led out the third hand with Triton, which set the theme and power of the round in the water suite, and in which Nike had no cards.

Her hands were practically shaking around her cards, and the round passed quickly.

Dave played a siren.

The next round, Dave played the sea monster card.

And on the last round of the match, Dave played Poseidon.

Nike stared at him, appalled. "I can't have lost to a mortal!" she said.

Dave shrugged. He folded his arms, playing it cool. "It was just lucky hands," he said. "The Fates were probably involved." He nodded at Zeus. "What he said."

Zeus roared with laughter. He laughed so hard the table vibrated, and even Hera started to chuckle. And finally, also Nike had to thaw and found the ghost of a smile.

"That was one of my favorite card games ever," Zeus said. "The way you disarmed the goddess of victory," he shook his head. "That was something else, Dave."

Nike sighed. She stood up, grateful to at least get away from the back of that blasted chair.

She was nothing if not a gracious loser, and she always honored the victorious.

"Congratulations," she said. "The winner of the game gets to petition the king of the gods for a wish."

"Oh," Dave said, looking flustered. "Great!" He stood up, and pulled his hat out of his back pocket, and, working it in his hands, bowed to Zeus. "I'd like to request safety and success and a general good time for me and my buddies when we climb the peaks."

Zeus smiled, and held out a hand in benediction. "You can have it," he said. "A man after my own heart. I love a good mountain top."

"I'll give you the gift of comfort on your travels, that you may enjoy yourself," Hera said. "Or at least as much comfort as possible for this kind of thing."

"And I'll give you the gift that you can make the journey and be victorious in your pursuits," Nike said begrudgingly.

"Thank you!" Dave beamed. "Thank you very much!"

Nike escorted Dave away from the table where Zeus was pouring himself another flask of the mead and Hera was standing and straightening her dress.

"Thanks for the game," Dave said. "You're a cool goddess."

"Thank you." Nike was hardly feeling gracious.

"But you—I saw how you wanted to win so bad," Dave continued. "What did you want to ask him for?"

Nike flushed. It hardly seemed decent that a mere mortal may have picked up on her intentions, let alone that he'd ask her about them. She felt both flattered and annoyed.

"I wanted a new torch," she said. "I'm the goddess of victory. My old torch is made of fire. It does okay. But I want another option that can be sleek, and modern."

"No kidding?" Dave asked her. "Wow, maybe I can help."

"How?" she asked him frankly.

Dave was already getting down on his knees and unzipping his backpack. "This manufacturer," he said, pulling out a ridiculously sleek-looking flashlight. "They're amazing. Take a look."

Nike accepted the sleek-looking flashlight from his hands. She had to admit it felt good to hold the thing—the contours were attractive and very touchable. There was a row of buttons, and clearly the flashlight could do different things— judging by the icons it looked like the options were broad diffuse light, focused beam, flashing light, and Morse code.

"It can clip onto a belt, and it also has a phone charger," Dave said.

"Thanks, but I don't have a phone," Nike said. "I don't need one."

Dave took the flashlight back and turned it on. "Hold it now," he said. "Like you would a torch."

Carefully, Nike took the flashlight back. She gripped it in her fist and extended it like a torch, and somehow the moment wrapped her in a fantasy.

It was an autumn night, and Nike, the goddess of victory, was jogging through a city park. The ground smelled of wet leaves, and the air had the freshness of a recent rain. Nike wore a track suit of a beautiful purple and the latest in structured athletic shoes. On her face, she wore her new sunglasses. The sleekness of the torch in her hand had an elegance that complemented the sunglasses. Her torch was lightweight, and easy to grip as she jogged along through the park. With the flashlight, she could send the light of victory where she willed. Now, rather than merely having a beacon of light that went up, she could have a directional light. She could pause beside a footrace and shine the light of her new torch on her anointed victor. She could watch a boat race from a shore and do the same thing. When she needed to send a message to encourage victory in one whom the Fates had decreed must win a race, and who needed Divine Providence to access their victory, she could send the coded message they needed into the ethers, using the power of the torch's beautiful embedded Morse Code function.

Nike shook herself, coming out of her fantasy.

"Wow," she said, catching her breath. "That looks actually really useful."

Dave smiled, his chipped tooth showing. "Keep it," he replied. "My gift."

He seemed to find humor in this moment, so she looked at him questioningly.

"My best friend Gregory things he's God's gift to the planet," Dave said, confidingly. "I just think it's real fun that I get to give a gift from the planet to the gods."

All right. That one did amuse her. A surprised laugh burst from her lips, and she could feel the tension in her chest relax.

After Gary had returned down to the temple, flashlight-less, and Nike had returned to her home, carrying the new torch that wasn't from Zeus, she schemed to herself how she would bring it next time, to the next game to which she was invited. She would sell Zeus on the idea of accepting it. He'd probably say yes. After all he was an ancient god coming more and more into modern times.

And besides, at the very least, she had a really good lemon bread recipe she could bake to try and sway his favor. Maybe before the game she could drop off a loaf with the Fates as well.

It couldn't hurt to try.

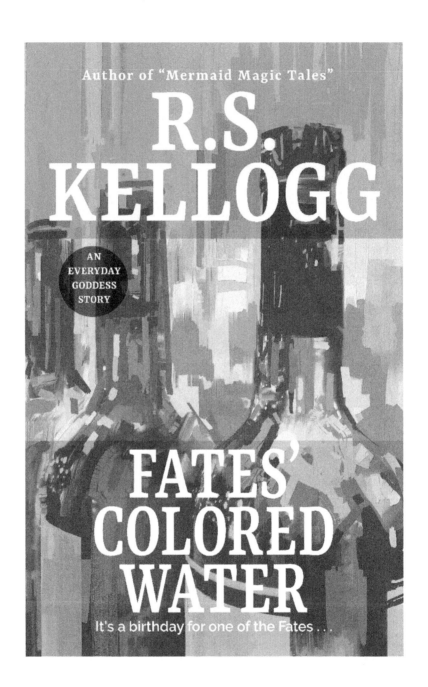

Author of "Mermaid Magic Tales"

R.S. KELLOGG

AN EVERYDAY GODDESS STORY

FATES' COLORED WATER

It's a birthday for one of the Fates . . .

Fates' Colored Water

by R.S. Kellogg

In the cave where the Fates spun, measured, and snipped the life threads of mortals and other beings, today was not business as usual.

Chloe, the spinner, had tidied up and put all the regular working tools away.

The silver scissors and orange tape measure had been careful stowed in a cupboard after being wiped down with lemon cleaner and dried on a soft clean towel.

The worn wooden spindle that she used when she spun the rough threads for common folk had been cleaned and put away in a tidy woven basket.

The shiny golden spindle that she used when she spun the finer threads of heroes and demigods had been stowed in a separate basket.

The ethereal white spindle that she used when she spun the finest threads of gods and elementals had been set into an urn with a picture of Athena on it, and the mouth of the urn had been covered by a geode. Nobody wanted to work with those threads until they absolutely had to. Out of sight, out of mind, Chloe always said. Maybe she felt a little queasy looking at the threads of the lives of beings who were the closest thing she and her sisters had to friends.

Skeins of threads of all types were carefully organized and put away for another day.

The walls of the workroom, embedded with relics of achievement through the ages, was bumpy and uneven—riddled as they were with the imperfectly incorporated detritus of years gone by. Chloe had carefully dusted the edges of things that noticeably protruded—the abacus edge near the entry way, strands from a wig which had belonged to a queen, a couple of trophies from great athletes, and the limbs of a statue depicting an eight-legged horse.

Sometimes she felt like her sisters incorporated into the walls the cast-offs of anyone who was notable that was dead including some folks who were a little obscure, but it was handy to have something visually interesting in the space when she felt bored with spinning.

The walls couldn't literally talk, but they made a pretty good pictogram.

Now, the great workroom sat empty.

It was Atty's birthday, an occasion to celebrate.

Lach had disappeared into the kitchen to get things ready.

Atty, who had been disturbingly morose lately, had disappeared.

Hopefully she would be back in time for the party tonight.

Hopefully.

Chloe had her fingers metaphorically crossed.

It wasn't optimal for the Fate who cut the life threads to be on a depressive streak, and Chloe really hoped today's party would snap Atty out of it.

The incense pot of the Fates released clouds of fragrant smoke as per usual, but it was not the customary blend that infused the space with the uplifting scents of tangerine and heavenly grace and the earthier scents of vetiver and other grounding aromas—a combination that the Fates felt helped them work with the dual sides of mankind, in their spiritual and earthier aspects. Instead, the pot was releasing scents of celebration. Eucalyptus, a favorite scent, as well as happy notes of rosemary.

The floor had been carefully swept and then frenetically scrubbed over with the good cleansing lemon-y soap, polished so it nearly squeaked with cleanliness. Sunflowers from a nearby meadow had been stashed in an urn depicting the muses and set on a doily that Chloe had crocheted, right at the center of the crafting table.

The only sounds in the caves right now were the mellow yowling of the wind outside the entrance-way tapestry, the crackling flames in the great Fireplace of the Beyond—an impressive affair of metal and pipes—and the sounds in the kitchen beyond the great workroom.

In the kitchen, Chloe joined her sister and picked up her knitting project. With the needles clicking steadily under Chloe's hands, she fell into a steady rhythm that offset the more irregular clatter of Lach bustling about the space making a spice cake for Atty. Lach was currently fiddling over the exact spice mix to include in the recipe. Chloe was wearing a pretty off-white dress under her apron to keep her party clothes clean. Lach wore a practical brown dress with a tan apron, and sensible brown shoes.

The kitchen, beyond the range of the caves where the Fates entertained guests and therefore under less pressure to appear historic and traditional, was cheerfully lit by warm-tone torches which the ever-practical Lach had augmented with a trio of overhead modern chandeliers and some recessed lighting. The torches in the kitchen had real fire, and were kept perhaps more for old-time's sake than anything else: a gesture toward their roots. All the other lighting was powered by electricity.

Chloe worked on finishing a delicate knit shawl. The needles in her hands felt comforting, and her fingers moved steadily, coaxing the yarn into the intricate pattern that would finish up the edge of this masterpiece. The shawl was a lovely shade of hunter green, and would be the perfect shade to set off her sister Atty's eyes.

Maybe that would finally cheer Atty up.

Chloe caught a whiff of cinnamon as Lach scooped out a generous measuring spoonful.

"Do you think this will work?" Chloe asked hopefully. Chloe left unstated the possibility that the party might remind Atty of the march toward her own, though-distant, eventual ending.

"It may or may not," Lach said placidly. "What matters is that we let her know that we care." She tossed a small measuring spoonful of cinnamon into her bowl of flour, and began to stir. "It's basically all we can do."

"It's been really jarring to me that her job has been . . . getting to her a little too much lately," Chloe said. "If this doesn't work, I may go on a holiday. For my own peace of mind."

Lach fixed Chloe with a steadying look, and Chloe sighed. She was well aware of Lach's opinion that of the three sisters, Chloe was the most lightweight. "If you need a vacation, you don't need to blame it on your sister in order to take one," Lach said.

Chloe shifted her shoulders back, feeling a bit stung. "Fine," she said. "Maybe I will. Maybe I'll visit Italy later in the season."

A clattering sound from near the cave entrance made Chloe jolt in her chair.

Lach frowned. "She's back early," she said. "Now the party won't be a surprise."

Firm footfalls coming through the entrance chamber and the workroom assured Chloe of one thing: Atty was not in a mood to be cheered up.

Sure enough, when Atty burst through the doorway into the small cave that served as the kitchen, she was still wearing the black turtleneck and jeans that she'd left the cave in that morning. Now, her face looked wan and pale even under Lach's modern lighting.

Lach squinted and frowned at Atty. "Is that Goth makeup?" she asked, and strode straight to her sister's side, flicking a finger up Atty's cheek and then frowning at the white face powder now on the tip of her finger. Lach tilted her head and looked at Atty, who reached to rub the streak on her cheek where the make-up had been removed—the area was now pink.

Chloe noted Atty's heavy eyeliner. "Did you go to a mall and get a make-over?" she asked, trying to make her tone as cheerful as possible. "That's a fun way to celebrate."

"I'm coming to accept my actual role in the world," Atty said, with dramatic flair. "I'm basically a goddess of death." She strode over to the mirror on one side of the kitchen and inspected her smudged make-up critically.

"Oh great," Chloe mouthed at Lach, who gave her a ghost of a smile, but shook her head, in a curt reminder not to do anything that might make Atty even more grumpy. Chloe quietly set her knitting on the table. There were bigger things to take care of at the moment, and besides, Atty definitely wasn't in the right mood for appreciating fine handiwork.

"What's set you off?" Lach asked, wiping her hands on her apron and coming to stand beside Atty at the mirror. Lach was a couple of inches shorter than Atty, but more solidly built, and a more comforting presence by half.

"I can't tell you," Atty sniffed. "It isn't very goddess-like."

Chloe and Lach looked at each other, and then Chloe stood and the two sisters headed towards Atty's room.

"No!" Atty cried, flinging herself toward the doorway of the room in an attempt to block them. "You can't know my secret."

Chloe noticed Atty was wearing some sort of new, dusky perfume, and wrinkled her nose. It was not a lighthearted scent, and it had a definite bitter undertone that warned people to keep away. Chloe imagined the perfume had some sort of a dreadful name such as "Nightshade" or "Prowler." She shook her head. When Atty was sad about something, she sure went all in.

"You got another crush, didn't you?" Chloe said, putting one hand on her hip. "And then he died, right? And you feel guilty about snipping the thread? Who was it this time?"

Atty flushed. "Well, it's different this time," she protested. "He isn't dead yet."

"What?" both her sisters said at the same time.

"What exactly is going on?" Lach asked.

Big tears began to spill from Atty's thickly lined eyes.

"Careful," Chloe said, "You'll spoil more of your makeup." She fetched a cloth napkin from the table and handed it to Atty, who blew her nose into it and handed it back to Chloe.

"Gross," Chloe complained, going and dumping the napkin into the dirty rag basket under the sink and hurriedly scrubbing her hands with the lavender soap that she'd originally purchased hoping it would boost Atty's spirits but now just served to remind her that her thoughtfulness toward Atty did not seem to be getting returned.

By the time Chloe was done scrubbing her hands, her two sisters had disappeared into Atty's room. So Chloe followed.

She didn't want to miss anything.

When she got through the doorframe into the dark room, Chloe stopped in her tracks.

In Atty's room, which reeked of patchouli, a shrine had been set up.

A shrine to a *mortal*.

It took up an entire wall.

Pictures cut from newspapers and magazines had been carefully pasted on posterboards and hung in a display. A substantial, ornate purple candle decorated with orange wax flowers and vines sat on a low table at the base of it all. The candle was not lit, but it rested next to an offering plate filled with various types of cheese.

Chloe recognized the man in the pictures more by his energy than by his face.

"Your taste's slipping. He's not even a hero," Chloe remarked to Atty. She'd woven his rough life thread a bit of time ago—perhaps a few months? It may have been more. Of course, goddess time and human time were very different things, and so at this point, the man was probably dipping toward death.

Or would have been, had Atty been doing her job.

Chloe frowned at the images and the news headlines on one of the poster boards.

"Old man Jerrold sets aging record at 127," read a prominent headline near the bottom. There was a picture of old Jerrold, his face lined and eyes twinkling, somehow still very handsome. His wrinkled hand in the black-and-white photograph gripped a bottle with a label that said "Youth Elixir." Well that was interesting.

Chloe felt the blood drain from her face as she turned to look at Atty, appalled. Atty had the good grace to look just a little chagrined, but she sniffed and lifted up her head, defiant.

"You can't just let them go on indefinitely," Chloe said, her tone shocked. "It isn't good for them. You have to let him go, Atty." She turned to her sister. "How long did you measure his life to be, Lach?"

Lach looked over the posters with a jaded eye. "Technically, this guy was supposed to expire about forty human years ago," she said. "What are you holding out for, Atty? Why not let him die already and move on? At least you'd have a cute ghost to moon over, hey? Can't be kind to keep him forever, is it?"

But Atty looked serious as she stared back at her sisters. There may have been melodrama earlier, but she was calm now. "You wove his thread from the commoner range, Chloe," she said.

Chloe shrugged. "Yes. He's a commoner."

Atty shook her head and frowned. "No, he is special," she said. "He deserves a legacy. He hasn't created one yet, so I'm keeping him around until he gets one."

Chloe smiled a tight smile, feeling a little defensive about her choice of threads for Atty's huge crush. She folded her arms. The choice of what kind of thread to pick out for each soul was a little subjective, of course, but she had a really good track record of matching the correct kind of thread to be accurate for each individual soul.

And it wasn't like heroes necessarily had longer lifetimes than commoners. If anything, they seemed more likely to go down in an early blaze of glory.

And if Atty was thinking that this guy had merited a thread from the skeins reserved for the elementals and the gods, she had another think coming.

Besides, there was always the loophole.

"You know, he's got the same power as anyone else," Chloe said, with just a bit of an edge to her tone. "If he's completed deeds noble enough to warrant an elevation, his life will transmute his own thread into something finer."

Atty pressed her lips tight together at that, and folded her arms around herself, clutching at the fabric of the sides of her turtleneck.

Ah, there was the catch.

Atty had fallen in love with someone she'd hoped would ascend and become a hero or some other being that deserved a better afterlife than being a ghost. And apparently, he hadn't lived up to her dreams.

"Where's the thread, Atty?" Lach asked quietly. She was staring at her sister with calm brown eyes. Calm with intensity underneath.

They'd been down this road a few times before, though it had never prevented Atty from completing her work previously.

It was dangerous for Atty to get a crush.

It could make it difficult for her to let go.

But always in the past, she'd simply gone dark and morose and wasted away after a dead cute man for a while after his passing. While her sisters pretended not to notice that she'd slip out at night for a few months to go flirt with some ghost.

It had been annoying, and made Atty a distracted conversationalist, but as long as her sisters kept a watchful eye over her, she could still do her job.

They knew to watch her very closely during these periods, as she might be inclined to mess with other life threads' lengths just out of spite. So during those times, Lach would tie a metal nut onto the thread just where Atty was supposed to trim it, and Atty would silently and passive-aggressively snip it at *exactly* the point right after the nut.

Eventually, the attraction would fade, or Atty would move on, or maybe the ghost would get assigned to some really wonderful version of an afterlife and not come back anymore.

And then Atty would sulk and then soften and be regular Atty again. Their usual, generous, high-functioning sister.

But Atty wasn't letting this one follow that typical cycle.

"Where's the thread?" Lach repeated firmly.

Atty shook her head.

"Show me." Lach's voice was like steel.

"It's . . . just there," Atty finally conceded. She pointed to a part of a poster board that had some incredibly handsome pictures of her crush when he was younger . . . alongside several news headlines which Chloe privately felt seemed hyped. The skein of thread for Jerrold had been tied with a red ribbon and placed like an offering on the floor beneath the poster.

It was still in its skein, and had a light mark where Lach had measured that the cut should be. Shimmering light coursing along the thread showed where his actual lifespan had moved beyond the cut mark by a good several inches.

Chloe bit the inside of her cheek hard enough that it hurt, and skimmed over the blazing headlines of the posters on the wall. Apparently, this guy was a healer to rival Chiron, with a wisdom on par with Socrates.

She wondered if Atty's crush had hired the services of a PR firm.

"The gods get crushes on mortals all the time," Atty said sadly, waving her hand despondently as if that justified everything. "They grant them favors. Why don't we goddesses get to do things like that as much?"

Chloe sighed. "What kind of favors did you grant this guy, Atty?"

"It wasn't much," Atty protested.

Both of her sisters glared at her.

"Okay, he was a doctor, a researcher," Atty amended. "I let him postpone death for other people if they asked him nicely."

"What?" Lach said, in a tone that was rising.

Chloe realized her face was hot. "You're basically undermining our work," she said, her voice tense. "I pick the thread and weave it for a particular purpose. Lach measures the thread and determines its length. You are supposed to cut the thread, Atty. How many threads have you not cut?"

Atty waved a hand weakly at another poster board, where she'd taped up more news headlines and pictures.

Apparently there was an entire enclave of very old people, headed by Jerrold, somewhere in Italy.

"Maybe you can go on vacation to Italy there, Chloe," Lach said grimly. "A working vacation. With Atty's scissors. And you can do Atty's work for her because she's clearly falling down on the job."

"Wait!" Atty said, stepping between her sisters and the posters. "You can't just cut me out like that."

"Well, if you're not doing the cutting then someone else will have to!" Chloe said, her fists tense. "Tell me, how exactly is letting that guy live forever going to help your cause? If he hasn't done something heroic already, I don't think he's going to come up with a grand invention in his one-hundred-and-twenty-eighth year!"

Atty grinned, defiant. "That's where you're wrong," she said.

"What do you mean?" Lach said, her tone quite a bit more edgy than her usual calm.

"I'm waiting to see if his colored water drinks pass muster with the current review they're under."

She pointed to a news article of Jerrold with a color photograph of him triumphantly holding up a bottle of his Youth Elixir. It was a strange shade of orange.

"Youth Elixir?" Chloe repeated, incredulous. "He was holding a bottle of that in another photograph, too. You've at least had better judgment in the past. How in Tartarus have you managed to fall in love with a snake oil salesman?"

Atty patted the leg of her jeans with her fingers and looked up innocently.

"You've helped him, haven't you?" Lach said flatly. "Somehow whatever's in that bottle must have come from you."

Chloe had started looking through the news photos of Jerrold more closely. She nodded to herself with disappointed satisfaction when she realized that Atty was visible in the background in at least three of them. In the color photograph where Jerrold was holding up his orange wonder drink, Atty had at least attempted to mask herself with an oversized pair of sunglasses and a big dark hat. But Chloe would recognize those angular elbows anywhere. And in another shot—the one of old Jerrold at the beach with his immortal colony, Atty was clearly visible to the side wearing—Chloe swallowed hard—a bikini with what appeared to be a skull-and-bones pattern.

"Traitor," Chloe muttered.

"So, what's in the bottle?" Lach asked, staring at Atty hard, who remained silent. Lach turned her ferocious concentration to the picture in the news article. The image was a bit grainy, but the texture of the beverage looked a little familiar. A bit sloshy on the sides, yet watered down—it struck Chloe that it reminded her of . . .

"It's the nectar of the gods," she breathed. "Atty, first of all, how could you, and second of all how in the heavens has Zeus not caught wind of this already?"

Atty, smug as a cat, looked down at the carpet, and Lach began tearing through Atty's drawers, looking for contraband.

"You look under her bed," Lach said.

Chloe crouched down on her hands and knees, peered underneath the thick black dust ruffle, the rough lace texture of it abrupt in her hands, sneezed at the dust beneath—Atty was definitely not as big on sweeping up as her sisters were—and then yelled "I found it!"

"We're all right here," Atty said witheringly. "No need to shout."

Chloe sighed, and sneezed again. She could see a huge row of bottles filled with golden-amber liquid that glowed softly in the dark. A slight shade difference from what was in the picture, but then she knew that newspapers weren't exact about matching colors for some reason. Probably a lower quality press than what the gods used for printing their internal circulars.

Kind of like how Atty herself had a lower quality of boyfriend selection than most of the goddesses who liked to date the occasional mortal.

She could smell, faintly, the unmistakable honeyed aroma of the ambrosia of the gods.

And the anxiety of her discovery made her stomach churn.

Lach drummed her fingers on the wall. "What are you having him mix it with?" she asked Atty, her voice tense. "It's orange in that photograph." She'd apparently reached a different conclusion than Chloe as to the reason for the difference in color between what was pictured in the news and what was clearly visible under the bed.

Atty tossed her head. "You're so clever, you figure it out."

Lach's brow lines deepened as she visibly churned through options.

Chloe, who was more of a hands-on goddess, went down deeper under Atty's bed.

"Wait!" Atty yelped, but Chloe's fingers had already closed around a bottle that wasn't glowing. She pulled it out and in the light they could all see it was a vividly red drink.

Chloe sighed. As she popped the top off, the drink bubbled up, bringing with it the scent of strawberries.

Taking a swig of the bottle, and gulping down a few swallows of the fizzy texture, Chloe nodded to herself.

She recognized a Hero's Elixir when she saw one.

Paying attention to the feel of the elixir as it settled into her system, she felt a boost come to her mind and to her limbs.

"I think this is a revitalizing mixture," Chloe said. "It's definitely one of Persephone's potions. Probably from her Sunshine line.

Lach's normal placid calm had bubbled over and she was clearly agitated. "So your plan . . . was to give this guy Jerrold a steady stash of elixirs of the gods, then let him feed it to himself and his friends to keep them feeling young and limber . . . while steadfastly refusing to cut any of their life threads . . . all while waiting to see if some clinical trials will prove that his so-called 'medicine' which is actually literally stolen from the gods passes muster with some scientists . . . in the hopes that Jerrold is deemed a hero, and his thread changes color, and he's sent to an elevated level of heaven where you two can have more fun hanging out together than the usual dank portion of the afterlife where you typically wind up visiting your old boyfriends?"

Atty shrugged in an offhand manner. "Something like that, yes."

Chloe sighed, setting the red fizzy drink on the bedside table. She noticed that her skirt was dusty, and leaned over to brush it down. The air in this room now smelled like a combination of dust and patchouli. Which, based on Atty's reasons for choosing past scents, meant patchouli was probably Jerrold's scent of choice.

Seriously Atty had the most aromatic ghostly romances of any goth goddess Chloe had ever encountered.

"I can think of some significant issues with your plan," Lach said.

Atty tilted her head and folded her arms. "Such as?"

"What will you do when Zeus and the others find out that you're supplying god-made contraband to some mortal crush?" Lach asked.

Atty flushed. "I'm a Fate. I'm above the purview of the gods."

"So was Cronos," Chloe muttered darkly. "Didn't stop them from taking him down."

"Don't you think they'll get angry?" Lach asked.

"If they're mean to me, I'll snip their threads." Atty replied.

"What do you think they'll do about Jerrold?" Chloe asked.

"What do you mean?" Atty sounded defensive.

"Do you remember the first time a mortal ended up introducing a tool of the gods for the betterment of mankind?" Chloe asked. "Remember what happened to Prometheus? I don't think things are going to go down very well for old Jerrold, even with the protection of one of the Fates."

"What do you mean, *one* of the Fates?" Atty asked warily. "If I support him, you two might be grumpy, but when it comes down to it, you'll support him too, right?"

The temperature in the room dropped by a noticeable few degrees, and the air between the Fates grew tense.

"Do not be so hasty to assume goodwill on our behalf," Lach said, in a voice that was ageless and deep, and so heavy that it could have sunken a boat.

Atty worked her jaw.

She looked first at Chloe, and then at Lach.

Neither of her sisters budged.

Atty's shoulders drooped, and she turned to look at the picture which featured herself and Jerrold on the beach.

She looked radiantly happy in her bikini in that photograph. Maybe the happiest that Chloe had ever seen her.

Atty reached out and touched the photograph, in the space between herself and Jerrold, who looked exuberant holding the bottle that was a gift from Fate.

"Just give me a week to wrap things up with him?" she asked.

"What happens after a week?" Chloe asked warily.

Atty sighed. "I suppose," she mused, "that it's time for me to let him go. I'd like a chance to say goodbye first, though. Of all the men I've ever known, *he's* by far been the most interesting."

Chloe glanced at a picture that featured Jerrold at a younger age, steering a small boat. The woman trailing behind him on jet skis appeared to be Atty.

"You have one week," Lach said, voice stern and unyielding.

She left the room, and upon her exit the temperature warmed up a few degrees.

"Chloe?" Atty said. She sounded truly despondent, and put a hand against Chloe's sleeve.

Chloe sighed. "What?" she asked.

"You believe me that he was worth it, right?" Atty asked. She sounded wistful, and Chloe reflected that of all the goddesses of the known realms, the Fates were somewhat unique among the immortals for never having taken long-term lovers.

Their work didn't really lend itself to long-term romance.

Chloe, irritated but compassionate, dug deep into her heart.

She saw her own fear that Atty might risk their safety and status, but also beneath that she recognized that she herself knew what it was to be lonely, and she could understand the impulse that might drive her more adventuresome sister out of the caves and into colorful relationships with engaging people.

She could see how she herself, given the right situation and making different choices, might have ended up in her own short-term romance with a human man.

Very short term.

Every human life was very short, relative to the Fates.

She didn't indulge in such things, but she could pity her sister who did.

"Make it a good week, Atty," she said. And she kissed her sister's cold powdered cheek, and turned around, and left.

Author of "Mermaid Magic Tales"

R.S. KELLOGG

AN EVERYDAY GODDESS STORY

HER
GREAT
LENGTHS

An unexpected adventure for Rapunzel . . .

Her Great Lengths

by R.S. Kellogg

The room at the top of the tower felt swampy with heat, and Rapunzel woke sweaty, her hair disheveled and her bed things kicked askew and strewn across the floor below.

The scent of day-old bread on the table reminded her that Mother had left the day before on an important errand, and was not yet back.

Rapunzel was still here alone.

Raising her eyebrows and working her jaw to the side, she calculated.

The sunlight shining through the thatched window was—let's see—probably at least halfway between dawn and lunch, and Mother had said that she'd return before dinner.

Which meant Rapunzel had half a day to herself, most likely.

Stretching her arms up above her head, she grinned. Luxury.

She felt guilty at the thought, but it was true.

Mother had been wanting to make applesauce and put it up in cans this week. Rapunzel got bored making applesauce, hated canning, especially disliked doing all of the above in the summer heat, and was grateful Mother had realized they were running low on canning jars—after Rapunzel's clumsy hands had broken three of them in the past month, as Mother had edgily pointed out. So Mother subsequently had business in town. Also, the labels Mother liked to use to make the jars look pretty were due to be delivered by Berta the peddler this week and had not yet arrived.

So joy was in order. Her sentence had been postponed, and the hot, sticky canning fate would wait.

Rapunzel pulled her night shirt up to expose the bare skin of her belly to the air and let her body cool off a little bit.

This barely helped, but at least it was a slight reprieve.

She tucked her arms behind her head, splaying her elbows wide, and stared at the demure gray bricks of the little arches in the ceiling above where she slept, where the edges of small notes that she'd written to herself were peeling away. Normally a square block of notes stuck to the ceiling greeted her when she woke up, but this morning there were two gaps in the spread.

Two of the notes had fallen down completely overnight. She found one next to her left ear.

"Keep going; you're doing a great job," it said.

After a bit of hunting, she found the other missing note on the floor next to one of her pillows, which had also fallen from above her bed. "Every day is a gift, what will today bring?" it said, with two little stars drawn next to it.

Mother was a big fan of uplifting saying—she always said that if the mind thought positive things, the world looked brighter—but Rapunzel was fairly limited in the range of what she could use for adhesives, and the rice-water paste she'd made had apparently not been up to the task of beating out the current humidity in the room.

As Rapunzel glanced up at the remaining cluster of notes on her ceiling, another one dropped away, following a zig-zag path to land beside her on the bed.

"I am enough," it said.

She half-grinned at the little doodled sunshine she'd drawn beside the delicate words—which she'd made as fancy as possible in curlicue font. Smoothing the curled corners of the note, she made a small stack of the three pieces of paper, and set them on the little kitchen table.

She could dabble with creating a better adhesive later today.

Lands, but it was hot.

Rapunzel flounced over to the great thatched window which overlooked the tower's clearing. Turning the little metal crank at the base, she circled it round and round as the gears made a little rappita-rappita sound and the great window swung open.

Drawing in a sigh, Rapunzel basked in the fresh air. The sunshine hit her square across the chest, but at least some of the staleness of the night was dissipating out through the great window.

The outside air was definitely not as humid as the inside air had gotten.

The tension melted from Rapunzel's back as she stood gazing out into the clearing and the trees beyond. She could hear the chirping conversations of the birds in the nearby trees—some of the trees that edged the clearing were lower than her tower, but many were taller. It gave a sense of decorous privacy, for her to have her home safely removed from the dangers of the woods, yet somehow still sheltered by them. The leaves rustling in the breezes fortified her for the new day, as did the grounding scent of green growing things.

A grin stretched across her face, and she opened her arms wide to all of it—the sunlight, the birdsong, the breezes, the trees, the fresh air, the new day.

All of it was hers, and hers alone.

For this rare occasion, she had the day to herself.

She giggled with delight.

And that was the exact moment she heard a knock at the door below: three sharp, impatient raps that sounded as if they'd been delivered by someone who had very sturdy knuckles.

Tensing, Rapunzel brushed at her wrinkled sleep dress—which did nothing to remove the wrinkles, and patted back her morning hair, which also felt like an exercise in futility.

She hadn't seen anyone come up the path.

Who had come, and how long had they been standing down there?

Was it someone Mother had been expecting? Evidently not, or she would have said something, or more likely she never would have left.

Could it be—gasp—a *stranger*?

A knock came again, louder this time. More determined. Not the knock of someone who was going to give up and walk away.

Rapunzel spoke with a voice that was higher than usual: "Who is it?" she called down. She realized her heart was beating rapidly.

"It's Berta, the peddler," called up a gruff female voice.

With a shuddering sigh, Rapunzel nodded to herself, feeling somehow—inexplicably—disappointed. It wasn't a stranger. She rolled her eyes at herself, wondering what kind of fantasy, exactly, she may have been hoping would play out here. It definitely wouldn't be good if she was confronted alone by a stranger. She'd have no clue how to handle herself.

"You're early," Rapunzel called down to Berta. "Mother wasn't expecting you for another day or two. Can you come back tomorrow?"

Berta grunted. "It's quite a hike to come all the way up here," she said. "Next time I come back around, may not be for another month. You sure you don't want to just accept this for your mother now, and we'll be good?"

Rapunzel's heart was beating hard now, and her eyes darted around the inside of the tower, from her messy bed to the tidy kitchen to the little library filled with books in the loft, to the door to her Mother's empty room.

This was a no-win scenario for Rapunzel, and she knew it.

Mother's rule was technically to never talk with strangers. But even though Berta wasn't a stranger, Mother was always the one who had dealt with her directly before.

It would probably be best for Rapunzel to send Berta away, and not to deal with her directly.

But Mother would probably be fuming mad should she return and determine that she'd missed the chance to get her precious labels from the peddler.

It didn't matter that it was no fault of Rapunzel's that Berta had shown up before Mother had returned. It would definitely still be Rapunzel who suffered Mother's anger if Mother got home and found out she had to wait another month before they could label the applesauce.

"Hmmmm." Rapunzel said, stalling. "Might be tricky for me to accept the labels."

"How?" asked Berta. "Just let me up, I'll drop them off, and I'll be on my way."

Rapunzel blinked rapidly, and pursed her dry lips, realizing she hadn't yet had anything to eat or drink today as she heard her stomach rumble. This was not an ideal moment for a visitor. Not that there was ever an ideal time.

Assessing the situation, Rapunzel decided that it was probably okay for her to talk with Berta, because Berta was Mother's friend. But letting Berta up and accepting the delivery was another matter entirely.

She couldn't very well let Berta come up into the tower without Mother being here—that would be even worse than talking to someone without Mother's permission. But Rapunzel had no way to get down out of the tower herself.

"Can you just set the box under a rock at the base of the tower?" Rapunzel said hopefully. "Mother will be back later today, and she can grab it then before I let her up."

Berta snorted. "Not on your life," she said. "I don't hand over merchandise until it's paid for. You know better than to ask me to do that, miss."

Rapunzel nodded, feeling guilty.

She glanced at the tin on the kitchen shelf where Mother kept the money sitting right there in the open. It was of little use to hide it, given that Mother and Rapunzel were the only two who frequented the kitchen. Mother had taken out a few coins to use for her errands in town, but the rest was here. Rapunzel never went anywhere, so she'd never had cause to use any of it before.

"What if I throw a few coins down for you?" she said, happy to have found a solution. "You can tell me how much it costs, I'll toss the money down, and you can leave the box beneath a rock. I'll even give you a little extra," she added. Maybe that would make everything all right.

Berta backed up the path toward the forest, and now she stood fully in Rapunzel's view, glaring up at her, one fist on her fat hip gripping a small box with a colorful fruit illustration on the outside, a fat bag on her back. Berta had thick eyebrows that nearly met in the middle, and she looked annoyed. Judging by the size of her bag, she had a lot of deliveries to make today.

"Your Mother may be my friend," Berta said, "But I know how to take care of my picky customers, and she's as picky as they come. What happens if I leave the box and it gets taken, or damaged in some way? You think she's going to be happy then? Not on your life. She'll demand payment back, and try to get a new, free box out of the deal as well. Do I look as if I'm made of money?"

Rapunzel glanced at Berta's outfit.

The battered boots, the short skirt that gave her a verisimilitude of femininity, which she wore perhaps a little ironically over tough pants which had patches over *both* knees, the tiny money bag which she wore on a string around her neck and tucked under her clothing, visible as a small bump on her huge chest.

Berta did not look as if she were made of money.

Quite the opposite, in fact.

"Come on," Berta said curtly. "Let me up, pay me for the box, I leave the labels, everybody wins. Okay?"

Perhaps it was one of the pitfalls manifesting from having been raised to be such an obedient child that led to Rapunzel finding herself nodding at this firm direction, hooking her hair onto the hook of the ceiling, and letting it down for Berta.

Berta, who had been up maybe twice before, when she'd brought a parcel of enough things that Mother had declined to lower herself down to retrieve them, tucked the box under the top of her shirt, left her bag at the base of the tower, and hoisted herself up the hair.

She was quite a bit larger than Mother, and Rapunzel winced as Berta hauled herself up and into the tower. Not that it actually pained her—the hook holding her hair bore the weight—but it didn't seem very kind to her hair to allow such a hefty person to put their full weight on it.

Finally Berta was in the tower, breathing hard for a moment after the exertion, standing hunched over with a hand on her leg. She straightened, and looked around.

Rapunzel discretely wrinkled her nose. Berta smelled horrible—sweaty, and muddy, and unpleasantly hot. Best to get this over with.

But before Rapunzel could scuttle over to get the payment and shoo Berta away, Berta collapsed down onto a kitchen chair, and popped off her muddy boots to Rapunzel's horror.

"Ah, finally," Berta said, splaying her stocking feet in front of her. There were holes over the toes on both sides, and the scent of Berta's feet was even worse than the sweat smell. "Rapunzel, be a dear and get me a drink of water."

Why was she doing whatever Berta told her to do? Rapunzel wasn't entirely sure, but she certainly didn't like it. She went without comment to the kitchen, where she silently retrieved a water cup and then fetched Berta a drink.

This despite the fact that she herself was thirsty and had not had anything to drink yet today.

She set the glass onto the table a little to the side of Berta, and the water sloshed a tiny bit—Rapunzel's silent protest over this whole situation.

Berta appraised her. "You look as if you just woke up," she said. "You want to get yourself a drink of water too?"

Rapunzel blinked. "Yes," she admitted.

"Well," Berta said, and made a shooing gesture toward the kitchen. Rapunzel retreated, fetched herself water, drank it in the kitchen, and then returned to stand near Berta.

"You really can't stay," Rapunzel said, concerned. "Mother is very particular about our rules here."

Berta grinned at her. "Wouldn't want you to get into trouble, kid," she said, and Rapunzel grinned back nervously.

The small stack of positive sayings with their tiny illustrations which Rapunzel had left on the table earlier caught Berta's eye.

"What's this?" asked Berta. She picked up the three little squares of paper as carefully as if they were delicate flowers, and gently riffled through them. "I am enough," she read aloud. "Keep going; you're doing a great job," she continued, and grinned. "Every day is a gift, what will today bring?" She straightened them together, tidying the edges so they all lined up, and considered the papers in her hand. "Dainty little sunshine there. I assume you made these? Very nice hand. Very pretty art."

Berta nodded to herself as if she were an expert in hand-drawn positive sayings and found these most satisfactory, and despite her awkwardness at having a stranger in the tower, Rapunzel flushed with pride.

"Thank you," she said, and pointed at the ceiling above her bed. "I find they're nice to wake up to."

Berta stood, stocking-footed on the floor, and padded over to look up at Rapunzel's full spread. Her mouth moved as she silently read the sayings aloud, pausing to consider each in turn.

Then, she turned to Rapunzel. "You have a gift," she said. "A very tidy design eye. I think I've found an artisan at sketching."

Rapunzel flushed again, feeling a little shaky inside, not entirely sure what this compliment meant, but glad to receive it nonetheless. She wrapped her arms around herself and stood there, biting her lower lip, uncertain as to how to move the conversation along, but still wrapped in nervousness at having another person in the tower.

Luckily, Berta had more experience with talking to people, and easily went back to the seat she'd pulled out from the table, settling herself down—the chair shifted under her weight. She set the three little papers she'd first commented on before on the table next to her, and picked up the box of labels.

"The box is two coppers," Berta said, and Rapunzel, grateful to have direction on how to proceed with the transaction, retreated to the kitchen, fetched two coppers out of the money jar, and returned with them to Berta.

"Here you go," Rapunzel said, putting the money on the table next to Berta's empty water glass.

"Thanks," Berta replied. "Can I have another drink?"

Rapunzel, wordless, scooped up the cup and returned to fill it up in the kitchen. It was cool and orderly in the dark corner of the tower that housed the small kitchen, and it smelled of soap, and herbs, and day-old bread. Here she could collect her thoughts a bit, and here the muddy scent of Berta was hardly noticeable. Why was the peddler not going already? She didn't like how comfortable Berta looked, sitting in that chair, as if she had enough attitude to stay camped there like a queen until Mother returned.

Rapunzel shivered to herself. If Mother got back and Berta hadn't left yet, Mother would definitely be very kind to Berta, but Rapunzel would definitely be on the receiving end of a long frustrating conversation afterwards.

There was no way that this day could end well. The earlier pleasure that she'd felt over Berta's compliments had faded, and Rapunzel had returned to her earlier baseline level of anxious dread.

It would probably be a little bit better if Berta was gone before Mother got home.

Rapunzel was distracted while filling the glass from the water cistern, and sloshed a little of the precious water on her own hand.

It was cold, and jolted her back to the present, and she dried her hand on the clean kitchen towel hanging beside the stack of plates.

She turned around to bring the water back to Berta, and felt hollow horror at the sight of the big woman placing a few items from her pack out on the table.

Rapunzel knew a peddler's sales spread when she saw one.

She felt the blood drain from her face. "I can't buy anything which Mother hasn't approved of," she said.

Berta looked up at her sweetly. "No harm in just looking, is there?" she asked.

Dropping her shoulders and head in defeat, Rapunzel sighed, and shook her head, and then she brightened. "Is that a bejeweled hair comb?" she asked, perking up and coming over to the table.

Picking up the comb in her broad hand, Berta offered it to Rapunzel. "They aren't real jewels, see?" she said. "That'd make it too expensive for a peddler of my station to haul about. They're shiny stones polished up and painted. But that's nice for peace of mind, right? If you lose a stone, you don't need to trouble yourself on it. Also, it makes the piece very affordable."

Rapunzel held the beautiful green comb, which was hefty for its size and seemed to have been carved from wood. It had wide teeth and little jewels—or stones, rather—outlining the shape of a heart on the base of the comb's handle. The jewels were red and a pale orange. The texture of the comb felt very comforting in her hand—a solid weight, so smoothly finished.

"What's it made of?" she asked.

Berta shrugged. "Don't know," she said. "Want to try it out?"

Shifting her weight from foot to foot, and realizing that she really shouldn't try the comb, Rapunzel felt a contrary impulse seize her.

She would.

She was going to comb her hair with this pretty comb that Berta had brought up.

May as well.

It wasn't as if she were going to be getting into any *less* trouble.

Starting at the bottom of her braid, Rapunzel worked the comb through the strands of her long hair, slowly working her way higher and higher up, luxuriating in how having a *new* comb to play with just seemed to make the whole experience a lot more enjoyable.

It had been a while since she washed her hair, and it smelled faintly of the light oil that she and Mother applied to it to keep the strands in place. It would typically have been another day or so before she undid the huge braid and washed and combed her hair again, but the act of combing out her own hair with this beautiful comb seemed just too good to pass up.

While she worked, Berta talked.

And the stories which she told delighted Rapunzel perhaps even more than the comb.

She heard about the bazaar in the nearby town, where Berta had haggled for her latest batch of wares, and where a man she was dealing with had offered to throw in the fancy comb as part of the deal.

And how Berta had glared at him—Rapunzel could imagine that the glare must have been formidable with those ferocious eyebrows—and Berta had told the man he was out of his mind as there were no fine ladies on her route who might appreciate such a find. Until she'd remembered Rapunzel, and thought maybe there was someone who needed to spend so much time on her hair that a pretty comb might be just the thing.

Berta told about the hills she'd clomped through on her route these past two days—the dogs at the house of a local woodsman had gotten loose, causing her some grief at one stop, and a farmer's wife at another home had tried to barter milk for canning labels, but Berta couldn't drink that much milk, had no way to carry milk with her and besides, it would go sour in the amount of time it would take Berta to return to town, so that was not a trade she could make (Rapunzel laughed at this, pausing as she combed through the middle section of her hair).

Berta told about the festivities of a summer peach festival at the castle, which she'd been privileged to attend, and about how all the ladies competing to be queen of the peaches had shown up in their finest dresses, with fancy hair and rouged lips—but here Rapunzel had to interrupt to ask what on earth were rouged lips, as she removed a few hairs from the comb and set them into the dust bin.

"Here, I'll show you," Berta said, as she riffled through the things in her pack, and came up with a small bottle. She set a small mirror against the bag so she could see herself, and then tapped a tiny amount of red powder onto the back of her hand. She then delicately blotted the red powder against her lips.

Rapunzel surveyed the results. "Those are redder than poppies," she said.

"I know," Berta said. "But it's all the rage with the young ladies, especially the ones who want to catch the eye of a young man."

"Oh, really?" Rapunzel said. "How much does it cost?"

Berta stared at her with a jaded eye. "I'm not selling it to you," she said. "Your Mother would certainly have my head, and I'd lose a customer. Also, where exactly would you be going to catch the eye of a young man?"

Rapunzel flushed and hunched her shoulders. "I don't know," she said. "It's just that if it's all the rage with the young ladies, and I'm a young lady . . ." she trailed off, wondering to herself why exactly she cared what other young ladies might think or what they might be doing—young ladies she had never met and likely never would see.

After a pause and a sigh, Berta took pity on her. "You know what else is all the rage with the young ladies? Beautiful hair accessories."

"Like the comb!" Rapunzel said eagerly.

"Yes, like the comb," Berta said. "Shall I sell that one to you and we can call it a day? I'll give it to you for a copper. I need to get back to my route, and I see you still have a ways to go to comb out all that hair of yours."

Rapunzel hesitated, comb half-way through her magnificent hair.

If anyone deserved a beautiful comb like this, it was her. She knew it. And somehow, she was hungry for this pretty thing in a way that she hadn't been hungry for something before.

"I can't," she said reluctantly, after thinking things over at length. "Mother would never forgive me. And also," she added, slowly. "The money is technically Mother's. I don't truly have a copper to pay you with."

Berta nodded, solemnly, and folded her arms, her brows knitting together in a thinking expression.

Rapunzel had the agitated feeling that Berta hadn't taken her refusal as a definitive endpoint, but merely a point to consider in their negotiations. She felt as if little butterflies were dizzily flying about in her innards.

Suddenly, Berta smiled. "I'm a barterer, miss," she said. "And I know just the thing." Winking conspiratorially, she scooped up the stack of the lovely positive sayings on the table beside her. "What would you say to the comb for a set of ten of these? I'll bet that I can sell these for a copper to the school teacher up top of the forest—she'd appreciate pretty things like this for her room. Or, barring that, there are a few young ladies in town that I think may enjoy something like these."

Rapunzel put a hand over her heart, which was beating wildly. "Do you think the other young ladies . . . might like my art?"

Berta grinned encouragingly. "Yes, I do think so," she replied. "I think they might like them very much."

The thought of her work being seen . . . being appreciated by these unknown peers of hers . . . it made Rapunzel feel a strange aching inside, but it also made her feel so hollow that it was painful. She reckoned she'd peg the feeling somewhere between deep yearning, triumphant happiness, and heavy loneliness. Her throat and upper chest felt heavy, and she nodded, blinking.

"Yes," she whispered. "I should like very much for you to take these to them." She sniffed, paused, recollected herself, felt her heart rate speed up to something closer to terror. "But you mustn't tell anyone who did these," she said. "Otherwise Mother will never let you come back."

Berta grinned at her, sympathetic.

To Rapunzel's astonishment, Berta stood up, and squeezed Rapunzel's hand warmly.

It was a shock to her system. The moment felt kind, approving, and supportive.

"They will never know who made these," Berta promised. "And you can have your lovely comb."

Squealing with delight, Rapunzel hopped up on a chair to select seven additional cards to pull down from her collection, calculating she could easily cut and draw some new ones prior to Mother's return. She felt wobbly inside. She'd have to explain the brush, the labels . . . it was a lot.

Her shoulders slumped.

And then they straightened at a thought.

Berta had said no one would know who had drawn the images.

And she clearly liked them.

"Berta," Rapunzel called from the chair. "May I ask an additional trade?"

"What?" asked Berta, all business woman.

"I'll give you three more of these if you'll set the box with the labels, along with the comb, at the base of the tower." Rapunzel paused, choosing her words thoughtfully. "That way, Mother can be happy that we have these things without needing to be angry at me for hauling you up into the tower. And also . . . that way I can enjoy the comb more because I won't have to feel guilty about it."

Berta, who had finished putting back on her boots, stood, folding her arms, head tilted to the side as she considered. "You've got yourself a deal," she finally said, and Rapunzel bounced on the chair for joy.

After Rapunzel had hastily re-braided her hair, and Berta had gone down from the tower, and Rapunzel could see the place near the tower where a light rock sat tidily atop a box of labels, with the comb beside it, she waited for her Mother as the light of the afternoon stretched toward evening.

As she waited, she hugged herself now and again and worked on her fresh art. She was still feeling delighted over the last thing that Berta had said:

"For a girl who lives in a tower, you're a pretty good negotiator. Just as good as any of the young people who live in the city."

She felt a pleased smile as she worked.

"Today is an amazing day," she wrote out, drawing images of happy sparrows all around the edges of a new card. She used blue ink to make cross hatching on the shadow of a tree that she added to the corner. And the letters on the beginning and end of each word got an extra-fancy curlicue.

Author of "Mermaid Magic Tales"

R.S. KELLOGG

AN EVERYDAY GODDESS STORY

THE QUILT OF THE FATES

Fate makes a craft project

The Quilt of the Fates
by R.S. Kellogg

Past a vine-covered cave entrance, which was hidden from all but the sharpest of eyes, in the craft room of the Fates, Lach had a headache. She'd looked a little too deeply into the red thread in her hand while preparing to assess and measure its life length, and now the headache was making it impossible to get into the regular flow of her work.

She set down the thread and the measuring tape.

The headache was focused in the center of her forehead, and she was fighting off the rising concern that she may need to take a break.

The craft room of the Fates, where the sisters Chloe, Lach, and Atty spun, measured, and snipped the life threads of mortals and other beings, was designed to be comfortable and supportive of long working hours. Having a headache—or any kind of discomfort, really—was so out of the ordinary for Lach that it had taken a moment for her to recognize it for what it was.

And she was having a hard time placing why it would be there.

The room, always a comfortable temperature, with a meditative ambient lighting that was neither the brightness of day nor the full dark of night, was suddenly beginning to feel a little too heavy to Lach.

The room smelled of textiles—cotton, and wool, and the dust of snipped threads and fabric. And the faint scent of lemon cleaner under that—Chloe was very big on making sure that the space was clean. Lach had little complaint with that, as she liked cleanliness as well. It was just that the scent of lemon felt a little loud right now. The incense pot of tangerine and heavenly grace and vetiver that always helped ground the Fates in their work seemed annoying to Lach as well.

The torches on the walls burned steadily, placidly one might say, representing the fires of lives that the Fates shaped in this space. Small lamps on the table provided bright spots of light for the sisters to see the necessary details work for their handicrafts, one of the small nods to modernity that the very traditional sisters had allowed to be included into their crafting room.

Noticing that her breathing was a bit ragged, and seeking calm, Lach focused on the sound of the trickle of a stream that flowed through the back of the caves, a steady friend to her work. It provided a soothing accompaniment to her progress day after day. The sound of the water made her feel a little bit better, but the headache was still there.

She glanced at the walls, which were embedded with eons worth of human and divine treasures from among the favorite lifespans of the Fates from among those who had passed on. Here and there an artifact was visible jutting out from the wall, adding what Chloe described as tactile interest. For the most part Lach had successfully coated the treasures embedded in the walls with layers of sealant, making the vast majority of the wall fairly easy to clean. But at the moment all that she could focus on with the wall were the small areas where things such as old parchment and tapestries and robes had been left unsealed—a successful campaign on the part of Chloe and Atty who liked to touch the soft things from time to time.

At the moment, the rising irritation within Lach, made her feel as if she could have walked over and torn some of these treasures out of the wall with her bare hands.

She took a deep breath, and set the thread aside which she had been measuring.

Placing both of her hands flat against the crafting table, she sighed.

What was off for her?

Lach prided herself on being a sensible voice among her sisters. Sometimes Chloe might come up with a fanciful idea to weave a thread for a life made out of cotton candy, for instance, but one raised eyebrow from Lach could be enough for Chloe to reconsider. Occasionally Atty might tip into the unproductive range of grim thinking as she endlessly trimmed the edges of life threads. But a few words from Lach would be enough to bring Atty back to center and back to work. Sometimes during Atty's most challenging times, Lach snuck recordings of soothing music into the room. This could put Atty into something like a working trance. But at least it kept her going.

(If Lach were one to pray, she would have thanked Zeus for the invention of modern music playing devices. Before their time, Atty's most troublesome moods had been headed off by Lach bringing in musicians to play.

But the musicians never seemed able to stay for long.

Something about watching the Fates work in person was a little bit much for any mortal musician. And even the divine ones got uncomfortable after a while and had to excuse themselves.)

So it was usually Lach who kept things going. Lach and her strong will and her implacable air, and the solid way she stood day after day on the shaggy carpet which she had procured to keep the sisters' feet buffered from the cold rock beneath.

Lach measured life.

She knew life.

And she represented the groundedness of the earth and its continual freshness and renewal to her sisters, and kept them all going, year after year after year.

She stared at the table which she knew so well and realized that if she needed to measure another thread just then she might scream.

A range of all the different types of threads that Chloe had spun and laid out for Lach to measure were making a blurry rainbow of colors before her, and her head was swimming as the colors of the threads danced before her eyes.

Must have been fifty separate strands of different textures on that table. Fine strands and rough strands. Polyester ribbons and chunky yarn. A delicate thread of gold had been laid out carefully at the end of Lach's line-up for the day—apparently for the lifespan of a royal princess.

Lach pinched the bridge of her nose.

Chloe had stepped into the kitchen for a drink of water. Atty was still morose and quiet after the death of her most recent human crush.

Lach needed a focal point that would keep her grounded, and she found it by staring hard at the ethereal white spindle off to the side of her table.

It was Chloe's supreme tool, her treasure. She used it to weave the silky threads of gods and elementals. Given that these beings were of such long and interesting lives, Chloe didn't use the spindle too often. But when she did, it lit up the whole space with a feeling of power, and creativity, and an almost electric sense of possibility.

Staring at the spindle, Lach felt her heart pounding and realized her mouth felt dry.

Was she unwell?

She was an immortal. Immortals rarely got sick, but she supposed it could happen somehow.

Lach realized she was swaying slightly just as Chloe came back into the room.

"Oh, my," Chloe said, bustling straight up to Lach and escorting her over to a chair by the Fireplace of the Beyond—an impressive affair of metal and pipes so ornate and sleek that it could have been made by Daedalus himself.

"You don't look well at all," Chloe said. "Sit there and let me get you some tea."

Chloe bustled out and came back soon with a cup filled with mint tea, which Lach sipped while staring at the fireplace and trying to get herself settled.

She traced the web of pipes and the ornamentations of mythological figures and symbols on the fireplace with her gaze as if she were walking a labyrinth to restore her peace of mind. By the time she'd finished the tea, she felt a little bit more settled, but also exhausted.

"She looks like she needs a good nap," Atty said behind her.

"I agree," Chloe said. "No more work for today."

Lach wanted to protest, but she found she didn't have it in her.

The sisters bustled Lach off to bed and had her tucked in within minutes, and Lach drifted off into sleep.

Two days later, Lach sat again in the craft room, on a tall padded stool, staring at the table.

Her headache was gone, but her will to measure the threads was also absolutely gone.

"Well, we do need to do the work," Chloe said. "Otherwise there'll be disorganization, a backlog on births, overpopulation, complaints from various gods and goddesses on all ends of lifespan management."

"We really need to get back to work if we want to keep flying under the radar," Atty agreed.

Lach didn't make a move to pick up the measuring tape.

"Can I measure it for you?" Atty asked.

Lach turned to Atty. "How do you manage, when you're feeling stuck?" she asked. "I understand I need to do my work; I just am feeling completely blocked on moving forward. Usually there's . . . a flow. I can sense what the thread wants to be before I pick it up. How long to make it. I can't sense it right now."

Atty frowned. "I could complain that you think I get stuck," she said.

Flaring her nostrils, Lach frowned. "I think you manage very well," she said. "I see you dealing with things and then getting to work anyway. How? How do you do it?"

Atty tilted her head from side to side as if working through an inner dialog. "So what you're saying to me is that you haven't felt blocked like this before?"

Shaking her head helplessly, Lach stared at Atty, waiting for any kind of insight her sister could provide.

With a thoughtful glance at Chloe, Atty scratched the side of her head. "When I'm stuck by the weight of my work, sometimes I just need a break," she said.

"I've taken a break," Lach said. "Two days. My headache is gone but my focus is also still gone. What do I do?"

"Should we try calling Athena?" Chloe asked. "She might be helpful with mental health care."

"I don't want to call Athena when this is something I haven't tried to figure out on my own yet," Lach growled.

Atty sighed. She drummed her black-fingernail tipped fingers on the table. "When a break doesn't help, I find a diversion or a creative expression can. How do I put this into steady Lach language?"

"I don't know," Lach replied wearily. "Just use your language."

"Well, I'm flattered you've asked for my help, don't get me wrong," Atty said. "I'm not sure you've ever tried to see the world the way I do, so bear with me. There's a lot of symbolism to our work, isn't there?"

Lach nodded to show she was listening, as Atty was clearly needing a reassuring response.

"We work with threads and spindles and scissors, but the work has . . . an invisible weight and a heft. It's filled with stories, really. Stories we can't unpack because it would take us forever, and besides—we don't really need to do that in order to do our jobs, do we? Just spin, measure, and snip." Atty grinned, a far-off smile that seemed to be directed at the work rather than at Lach. "Sometimes when I'm snipping the threads, though, I sink into it a bit more and I see everything. There's this divine life-filled pause where I see the whole thing—from the moment of a human's birth, to the glory of their infancy, their growing up years, their golden moments and their pains, their heartaches and heart joys and loves and losses and what they build within their lives and what they still desired. I see it all, Lach." Atty's gaze focused on Lach now. "It's big. It's full. I see the whole thing, and then . . . my scissors must fall. Because I am the one who brings endings. Sometimes, even though I don't see a whole life very often, I have to go and do more than just snip the lives. I have to go meet one of them and see them . . . to have a chat with them about the adventures of their lives—just to see that they're really real. Or sometimes, I need to make art about them."

"The collages on your walls," said Lach softly.

Atty nodded. "It helps me make sense of my work, I suppose," she said. "It helps me celebrate it, but also feel as if I'm in the right relationship to it—I make art and I make visits as my form of reverence and communion, I suppose. But rather than how the humans seek to commune with the divine, I'm seeking to commune with humanity, and with my work, and the sacred nature of what it is that I do. I'm a capstone, really, a culmination, a celebration. As long as I stay in that headspace I do okay. It's when I tip into the feeling of the heaviness, or avoid being present with my work, or simply get lost in the baggage of staring into occasional life after life whilst feeling disjointed from all of that where I get into trouble. I need to feel alive Lach. I feel alive through my work. And the way that I do it may look different than the way you'd do, but it works for me."

Atty patted Lach on the shoulder. "I can't say for certain what's going through that very practical mind of yours right now, but based off of how I see you behaving, and how I know my own patterns, I just wonder if the weight of the work has hit you in a way it may not have before. Maybe you need a communion too."

"A communion," Lach said. The words felt strange in her mouth but not unpleasant.

Had she been keeping herself separate from her work in some way?

She wasn't sure.

As far as she could tell, she had been completely present with it, as she'd always been.

But something had happened a few days ago that had clearly affected her more deeply than anything recently with her work had done.

And so she turned back to the table, with its scents of textiles and faint background smell of lemon cleaner, and she stared at the threads before her which were waiting to be measured.

She'd always gone by weight and by sensing before, feeling into how long any particular thread wanted to be, and then snipping it.

But now she turned back, to the particular thread that she had been about to measure when the headache had come on.

A red thread.

As she picked up the measuring tape once again, and then went to pick up the thread, she felt a whisper of the headache return.

"What's going on with me?" she whispered.

In the background, the stream trickled on, and the wind blew blearily beyond the tapestry and the vines that blocked the entrance.

"It's possible that this particular thread is what's needing communion," Atty said helpfully.

"That's very vague," Lach said archly.

"Do you think it's seeking communion with her or she's needing communion with it?" Chloe asked.

"Don't know," Atty said. "Might not matter. It's just the recognition that matters."

Lach reached for the thread slowly. She noticed as her hand drew closer to the thread that her headache picked up, and as she pulled her hand away her headache died down.

She frowned. "I have never had this experience before," she said.

Atty shrugged easily. "Let's find a way to work with it," she said. "How would you recognize this life? Want to go talk to the guy?"

Lach checked in with herself. No, she didn't share Atty's interest in chatting with mortals.

"What if you did a craft?" Chloe said softly.

"What, like tied a life thread up into a bracelet?" Lach said. "That would go over very well with the gods."

"Not a craft with it," Chloe said. "A craft about it."

Lach, who at this point had shrugged off the notion that she'd be able to easily flow into the work day in her usual fashion, seriously considered this idea.

How would she make a craft about a life?

About a life that had enough energy to it that it gave her a headache to contemplate picking up the life thread of that life?

Any of the sisters would come up with a different way, so she didn't dare ask her sisters for their ideas on this point. She was the one who was having the headache. She needed to come up with the Lach way of communing with a life.

She glanced around the craft room.

Scissors. Threads.

The answer landed with her silently

"I'd like to make a quilt," she said. And in the cave, her words seemed to fill a need that had previously gone unexpressed.

A quilt.

The sisters all nodded.

It did feel as if the red thread was hungry for a quilt.

So Lach went with Atty as a guide to a human fabric store, feeling some strange kind of kinship amongst all the people who shopped there, mostly older women who had gathered to examine fabrics and notions and lace, and threads, and choose things that went well together, and put together their orders. She felt as if she were a senior member of a very well-established club, the club of the crafters.

Somehow, she knew exactly which fabrics to buy for her quilt.

When she went to get them cut, the ladies at the cutting station patiently worked through dozens of different materials.

"Making a crazy quilt?" one of them asked.

"Just to help me work through some things," Lach said, perhaps a trifle defensively.

"Lady, I hear you," the lady measuring the fabric said appreciatively.

Lach noticed approvingly that the way she measured the fabric was skillful and professional. "You're good at your job," she said.

"I enjoy it," the woman replied. "Besides, it gives me a chance to hang out here."

Lach glanced around at the rows of bolts of fabric and the seasonal décor. Even though it was impossibly far removed from her caves, and the tone here was much more light hearted, something of the feel of it was the same. The feel of potential, of creation.

"I understand," she said, and took the large stash of cut fabric.

Atty, who somehow unsurprisingly had human money on hand, paid for the material at a different spot, and the two of them left.

While Lach worked through her quilt-making process, she set the red thread beside her and looked at it deeply as she went.

The patches she chose and trimmed and measured with exactness fit what she felt in the red thread.

What caught her off guard was that there were so many unexpressed emotions of the woman whose life the thread embodied.

Unexpressed desire to be on a sailing team as a young woman—Lach chose a deep fabric of blue with little gulls flying.

Nervousness at speaking in front of a class—Lach chose a fine-print pattern of tiny dictionary words.

Deep love for a partner that could never be fully expressed—Lach chose a burgundy shade with little white hearts.

Honorable service in as career as a teacher—Lach picked a patterned print that had little books.

A deep struggle with words to express affection for a sister—Lach picked a print of florals that seemed to her to speak of love.

The project went on for days, with Chloe carefully continuing her own work of spinning threads in the background—making things ready for the time when Lach would return. Atty, with no measured threads to trim, watched quilting videos to learn how to help Lach put her project together, and went out on her own to the craft store a few additional times to purchase a sewing machine and the right kind of batting and thread.

Finally, Lach started sewing her pieces together. After a few false starts, and after pricking her thumb on the sewing needle and needing Atty to get her a bandage, the thing began flowing together.

When the quilt was finished, the Fates hung it on the wall among the other artifacts.

It was the first piece to be included that one of them had made themselves.

"It has so much passion and heart to it," Chloe said softly, touching a panel of stars.

"I think you really did a good job," Atty said.

Lach said nothing, and the other two took a step back as Lach took a step forward.

She placed her hand against the soft center of the quilt. In her other hand she held the red thread, still waiting to be measured and cut.

It felt as if another person stood beside her, the woman whose life was in the thread.

They stood together, and they watched this life flow by, scene after scene, moments shared with others, and moments spent alone.

Things which had never found words or means of expression poured out of the quilt of this woman as if breathing relief.

It was all in the quilt.

When they got to the end of the story of this life, Lach felt down the red thread. She didn't need the measuring tape. She knew exactly where it was right to have it be trimmed. Marking the spot with her thumbnail, she handed it off to Atty, who nodded and silently retreated to snip the thread.

Tears were streaming down Lach's face.

She had never cried for a mortal before.

Beside her, invisible to the other two sisters, who had returned to their work at the craft table, the shade of the woman stood clear as day.

"Thank you so much," she said to Lach. "You saw me. And you saw everything I wanted to say and couldn't."

"It's been my honor to be your witness," said Lach. "You've lived a beautiful life."

The woman smiled at her. And in that moment Lach knew that she'd felt truly seen. And Lach felt, somehow, as if she'd been seen as well. As if her work, in that moment, had been transformed into a greater level of deepening and richness.

The shade faded away to continue to the next part of its journey.

But Lach kept the quilt up on the wall. She didn't even put sealant over it.

It wasn't often that she'd been able to commune so deeply with her work, after all.

The incense pot of the Fates sat in the corner of the craft room, releasing clouds of fragrant smoke to suit the work of the crafters. Tangerine and heavenly grace balanced the earthier scents of vetiver and other grounding aromas—the blend helped the Fates work with the dual sides of mankind, in their spiritual and earthier aspects.

As Lach thoughtfully went back to work at her table, groaning softly to herself at the sight of the huge backlog of threads, the tangerine and vetiver scents really stood out to her.

Human and divine.

All of her work was about the blend of life—spirit and its incarnation into form.

This vibrant thought radiated throughout her form so strongly in that moment that she couldn't breathe.

Then she glanced over at the quilt.

Mentally thanked it for teaching her to notice more deeply.

And returned to pick up the next thread on the table. This one was a delicate golden thread. Apparently Lach would get to measure out the lifespan of a princess this morning.

Human and divine.

A new peacefulness had settled over her, but also a new level of compassion and gratitude.

Lach smiled.

She picked up the golden thread on the table, feeling its metallic texture with her calloused fingertips.

It was time to get back to work.

The Quilt of the Fates

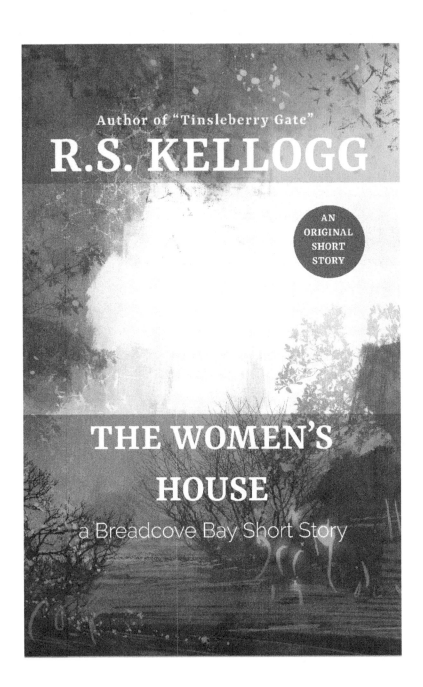

Author of "Tinsleberry Gate"

R.S. KELLOGG

AN
ORIGINAL
SHORT
STORY

THE WOMEN'S
HOUSE

a Breadcove Bay Short Story

The Women's House

by R.S. Kellogg

The Women's House didn't look like much from the outside.

Velli stood just inside the front garden gate of the small gray building on the corner of Pines Street.

It was located, improbably, toward the edge of the Central District of Breadcove Bay—the busiest part of the city, where most buildings stood three to five stories tall, shoulder to shoulder with no gaps between.

The Central District was a center of commerce and the arts, and the single-story Women's House, tucked away in its garden toward the edge of all the busy-ness of Pines Street, felt as if it were some kind of a sanctuary. There were no murals on the outer wall as there were on several destination buildings in the Central District, and it was painted gray rather than the customary Breadcove Bay white.

In fact, it almost blended in with the gray shadows of the tall pines and oak trees of its garden.

That was another thing that made it stand apart.

Very few of the buildings in the Central District had much of a garden, let alone huge trees.

The garden for the Women's House was much wider and deeper than the house itself.

As she stood in the sanctuary of the garden, slightly removed from the busy-ness of the street with its zip and hum of sleds of all sizes, the voices and footsteps of passers-by, and the more distant sounds of a train and of construction from a block over, Velli mused that she'd expected the Women's House to be larger, based on the stories she'd heard from other women—her sisters, her neighbors, her friends—who talked about it in hushed voices and glowing terms.

She was looking for deep reassurance, and healing from the grief which still weighed heavily at her shoulders, her throat and her heart, and she rubbed her brow wearily, wondering whether this small gray building could live up to its whispered reputation and possibly help.

Her cousin had died over a year ago, and grief still sat with her heavy, though she hadn't even managed to yet cry.

The air felt a little bit humid, and Velli smelled pine and the other scents from the nearby trees and shrubs and plants of the garden which flourished in front of the Women's House.

It seemed whoever kept the gardens here had a fondness for plants that smelled good.

Velli didn't know plants very well, but she was almost certain some of what was growing in the garden were herbs— only about half of the plant life in the low planters were flowers. The philosophy of whoever had planned the space was very different than that of the gardener back at home, who felt that beautiful women needed to be surrounded by beautiful flowers and sweet things in order to keep their temperaments sweet.

Velli kind of liked the variety in this garden here, though.

Some of the plants looked downright spiky.

Velli felt hot enough that she had removed her pale pink scarf and had tucked it into the pocket of her pale green jacket.

She hadn't needed an overcoat today—it was warm enough without one.

As there was no forecast of rain, Velli wore a small straw sunhat adorned with white flowers.

She had wanted to make a good first impression for the people at the Women's House.

The household sled driver had been busy today taking the first wife, Memmi, out on her weekly errands, so Velli had taken a train to get to the Hub Station nearest the Women's House, going by a map of the city to find her way to this place which she had heard much about but hadn't yet seen for herself.

She was the first of the wives from the household of Magistrate Starring to come to the Women's House, but the others would be eager to hear of her experience.

The path up to the door was made with pebbles; the yard all around it was dirt and growing things. There were a few benches here and there—sensibly placed not far enough from the path to be lost in the foliage, but with enough distance from the path to allow people to retreat to a bench for reflection, should they so desire.

Velli smoothed her skirt with one hand.

There was nothing for it.

Nobody was in the yard to direct her how to proceed, so she carefully, jauntily, walked up the path, her high-heeled boots crunching against the pebbles.

As she reached the front door, she heard gentle harp music drifting through a partially opened window, which sat above a fully stocked flower box.

Taking a deep breath in, Velli rapped on the front door with the back of her hand, a wild lightness surging through her.

The curiosity to see what it was like inside was climbing within her.

It was a few long moments before the door to the front of the house swung open. Moments during which Velli mused on the nature of her visit.

Would they be able to help her?

Was it even worth her time to come, other than potentially getting some good story material for the other wives?

She heard the unmistakable sound of a door unlocking, and the door swung open to reveal a kindly faced woman in a long gray dress, who wore a beige apron over the top of it.

The woman's hair was piled up atop her head in a tidy but messy black bun.

Velli hesitated.

The woman's gray clothing and her hairstyle marked her as being of the lower or middle class, but Velli had been assured by her friends that women of all ranks were welcomed here.

"Can I help you?" the woman asked. Her voice was pleasant and warm, if a little detached. It was clear from her tone that she wasn't taking anything for granted. She was neutral enough to field Velli whether she was visiting with a solicitation, or asking for directions, or any other reason.

"Can you help me?" Velli asked. "I've come to the Women's House to ask for relief from grief."

The woman nodded pleasantly as if this were nothing out of the ordinary. "Have you an appointment?" she asked.

Velli was taken a back, and hesitated. She hadn't heard appointments might be necessary.

"No," she replied.

The woman grinned, somewhat sympathetically, Velli thought. "Well, I do happen to have a gap later in the afternoon," she said. "If you can come back around three after noon, I can see you then. Would you like that time?"

Velli paused only a moment.

It would mean taking the later train home, but she could still swing it. She'd need to take a later supper with her children, but the staff at her house could take care of them until then.

"Yes," she said. "I'll take that time."

"Very good," the woman said. "I'm Fira, by the way."

"Nice to meet you, Fira," said Velli. "I'm Velli."

Fira fetched a log book from next to the door. She scribbled a few notes into it, then gave Velli a smile. "I'll see you later on today," she said, and carefully shut the door, locking it behind her.

Velli blinked.

Now she would need to find a way to spend a couple hours.

She found an eatery up the street where she enjoyed a savory soup for lunch, the familiar squeeze of grief still present with her lungs with every sip of the soup.

What might it be like to be free of the grief?

She shook her head.

What possible tools might Fira have that could help something as insubstantial as grief, anyway?

The Block Doctor at home, who worked exclusively for the health and optimal well-being of five Magistrates and their families, had warned Velli that the only way to deal with this kind of grief was to allow it to have its way with her, to run its course as if it were a stream.

He'd given her a kindly pat on the shoulder and told her to bear up.

But to Velli, the weight of grief had come to feel insufferable.

She felt as if in some way, the bond she'd shared with her cousin, who she still grieved so hard, was like an anchor chain, with the anchor being bound to him.

In some inexplicable way, Velli sensed that the bond was pulling her out of this life.

She couldn't speak the words aloud to the Block Doctor.

She couldn't speak them to her husband, the Magistrate Starring, as kindly as he was.

But one day, the youngest wife of one of the neighbors had found Velli when she was sobbing in mindless grief in the back of her orchard, and had carefully offered a handkerchief, and a whispered story of the Women's House.

The neighbor had never gone to it herself, but it had helped her friend.

And after that, Velli had asked around.

Several women, it seemed, had heard about the Women's House or had gone there themselves.

For nameless problems, wordless ones they couldn't put solid names or symptoms to.

Ungrounded feelings that couldn't find rest.

Unrequited longing or grief or frustration.

Deep lethargy that no Block Doctor's medicines could help.

Somehow, the stories always went, whatever was needing tending within the realm of what a woman carried within her heart, or on her shoulders, or within her mind—the Women's House could sometimes soften things enough to help.

At least enough to keep life bearable, to keep from checking out from it emotionally.

To keep a woman going, with her heart, and her shoulders, and her mind still accessible for both herself and other people.

Velli had a little hope from these stories.

She finished her soup, and folded her napkin, as tidily as she could—the way which she'd been taught when she'd been trained as a hopeful candidate for a role as a high-class wife.

The proprietor of the soup shop smiled at Velli as she left.

She smiled back at him in return.

She was a delightful presence that graced any room she was in, even with the almost palpable sense of her grief.

Of course she was.

She had been trained to be.

Velli spent time in a little dusty bookstore—so different from the wide, sunlight one she usually frequented up near where her home was—but she made a couple of good finds, and purchased one of them, a book about a pair of lovers which looked entertaining enough and which she felt privately might give her new material for fascinating Magistrate Starring.

It was always well to keep things fresh with him, and he enjoyed that she was a reader.

Velli returned to the Women's House at the appointed time with her book wrapped in brown paper and tucked into her over-shoulder bag.

Fira must have been near the front door, for she unlocked it and opened it as soon as Velli knocked.

"Come in," Fira said warmly. "You are welcomed in this place."

Velli thanked Fira, and came inside.

The Women's House smelled like lavender and jasmine.

The interior of the building was divided into multiple rooms.

The front area was small—just big enough for a bench and a basket and another basket with house shoes.

Velli removed her high-heeled boots gratefully, and slipped on a pair of house shoes in her size.

"What brings you in for a visit?" asked Fira.

"I'm looking for help," Velli said. The words she had come here to say felt heavy on her chest, and her voice felt constricted as she ached to say what was there for her to say. "I lost somebody very dear to me a year or so ago," she said, her voice sounding dull to her own ears. "The relationship was complicated. But I can't seem to let go of it at all." She placed a hand to her chest. "My heart aches every day." She bit her lip and took a shuddering breath. "I'm looking for help with finding peace, and some measure of healing. I've heard that at the Woman's House you help with healing wounds to the heart and the soul. Do you think you might be able to help me?"

Fira's face looked solemn. "I might be able to help," she said. "A bigger question is how much you are ready to heal."

"I think I'm ready," said Velli. She stared at Fira's dark eyes. "How would I know for sure?"

Fira smiled kindly. "The shape of every person's grief is quite different," she said. "So is a person's path through every kind of grief. Much of what is there is deepening for us, and some of what is there helps us honor those who have passed on. But depending on what is going on with your particular map of grief with this particular person, there are probably things which you are ready to shift or let go of—a process that happens in stages. So, can I help you today? Probably I can help you feel somewhat better. But will all your grief go away after today? Probably not yet." Her eyes looked solemn, but so filled with love and compassion that Fira virtually glowed. "The nature of grief is that it ebbs and flows."

"I'd be grateful for any relief," Velli said. She was okay with any shift toward greater ease.

"Well then," Fira replied. "Let's talk."

Fira guided Velli into a small, comfortably warm room. A window spilled dappled sunlight across the floor, and two comfortable padded rockers sat in the space, along with a bassinet, and a table that held an unlit candle and a few small bowls.

The room smelled of rosemary and lemon, and had a clean, cared-for feel to it. Velli didn't see any dust. She could hear the sound of the edges of tree branches tapping against the window in the breeze.

Velli smiled to herself. It was a welcoming room.

She turned her attention to the small table, with its two bowls.

One of the bowls was filled with what looked like sand, and the other was filled with water.

Fira held up a finger for a moment of quiet, and closed her eyes, mouthing words quietly to herself.

She lit the cantle with a small hand-lighter, and set it on the table next to the bowls of sand and water.

Fira had Velli sit on one of the padded rockers.

It looked well-used, but also well-loved, with a polished sheen to the wood, and the padding carefully stitched where there had been a repair.

Then Fira pulled the table next to Velli.

She placed on the table in front of Velli two small stones: A white stone and a gray stone.

"Choose a stone," Fira said, and Velli picked up the white stone, cradling it in both her hands.

The rock was flat with rounded edges, and it felt cool to her touch.

"Tell more about the person who you lost," Fira said, taking a seat in the second rocker. "Tell the stone in your hand. Who were they? And how did you lose them?"

Velli swallowed, and sank in on herself a little bit, details which Fira's keen eyes seemed to take note of.

"He was my cousin, Deruth," Velli said. "We were close our whole lives, until I married Magistrate Starring and . . . well, you know how it goes for high-ranking wives." She laughed her society laugh, and Fira looked at her sharply, seeming to instantly hear the shallowness of Velli's mirth. "We center our lives around our husbands," Velli said. "I didn't see Deruth much. And then a year ago I was invited to his funeral." Her voice had gone hollow, opaque. She didn't know herself here—she'd accessed some part of herself that was vulnerable, and raw, and that she'd kept clenched down inside herself tightly to avoid examining, in case she'd be burned by the heat and the charge of it.

The funeral hall had been long and claustrophobic.

Many visiting dignitaries had been there that day—such a colorful range of different tunics and capes of the different high-ranking houses. Even people in uniform from the rail station and the trades, and a smattering of the middle and lower classes had been there in the grays.

But what had stood out to Velli was all of the color of the upper-class families.

The stuffiness of the hall had felt a little suffocating.

The accusing, sad glare of Deruth's mother had made it even harder to breathe.

Velli had walked up that entire narrow, insufferable room with a clenching feeling at her throat, and had walked all the way up to the coffin, to her seat of honor nearby as one of his best friends.

The stiff, starched funerary clothes that Velli wore chafed at her arms and her neck.

The necklace that Magistrate Starring's head wife had loaned her for the occasion to help make a good showing for House Starring felt inappropriate given the childlike and mostly sunny quality of Velli's friendship with Deruth. She heard a few women murmur when they saw her wearing the necklace as she walked up to the front of the room, and she could sense that her presence, her status, the value of the jewels brought an aspect of respect to the proceedings, as they were meant to do, but all she could focus on was how the necklace felt so heavy, heavy enough that it seemed to her it would make her drown if she tried to swim in a lake.

She'd been assigned to sit at the front of the room next to Deruth's mother: Telluli, who had smiled at Velli but dug her fingers into Velli's wrist when she'd taken her hand.

115

Had leaned in with a smile to whisper to Velli, "You did this to him. You and I both know it. You were his heart and his world. His best friend. Then you disappeared. How could you have done it? You were his stabilizing influence."

Velli had blanched, both at these unexpectedly harsh words, and at Tellulli's breath, which smelled of chocolate and a hint of liquor.

Schooling her features quickly, as she had been taught to do, Velli had whispered in return, "I'm very sorry for your loss. I can see you are grieving very hard. It is a terrible loss, and I will miss him forever."

She was trying to be diplomatic, but Telluli had seemed vindictive rather than soothed. "Yes, you will miss him forever."

Velli had felt the grip of Telluli's fingernails on her wrist digging in, and something heavy had settled over her shoulders then—almost as if the full weight of this mother's blame for her son's death was settling hard onto Velli.

Velli had gasped, and found it difficult to draw breath.

Smiling, Velli and withdrew her wrist, and settled into the seat next to Telluli.

After the service, she had nodded like a doll at the never-ending line of people who came by to give their condolences to the family and close friends, and had listened to so many of them congratulate her on being such a comfort to Telluli that it had eventually set her teeth on edge.

She had kept her replies to people in a low murmur, as she had been taught to do in such a circumstance as a high-ranking wife.

The shame and intensity of the memory brought high heat to Velli's cheeks, and she felt as if she were going to cry.

She squeezed the white stone.

It seemed to be trembling.

Velli couldn't tell whether the trembling was coming from within the stone or from Velli's own body shaking.

Rocking slowly on the rocker, pushing herself contemplatively with her feet, Velli felt anger, stress, anxiety, and maybe, somehow, Telluli's blame spiraling out of her and into the rock.

"I feel so sad about losing him," Velli said. "We were so close. And I hadn't spoken with him in months beforehand, even though he'd written me to ask to meet up." She clasped her hands together tightly, and sighed. "His mother blamed me entirely for his death."

Silence lay in the room, comfortable and easy. A silence that welcomed Velli to say more should she like, or to remain silent for longer if she preferred.

In the silence, Velli felt the words she had just spoken hang low in the air.

His mother blamed me entirely for his death.

The accusation, the remembrance of the fingernails and the hot hand on her arm, all of it seemed to hang together for a moment, the words in the air and the memory of Telluli's blame gripping Velli.

Velli felt how the accusation, the gripping, were also connected up higher on her body—they pulled at her throat.

She remembered the weight of the necklace at the funeral—which had also been wrapped around her neck.

Fira simply gazed at her in compassion, rocking in her own chair. She nodded, companionably, as if the two of them were simply two ladies rocking alone together on a porch somewhere, with nothing heavy or of serious consequence to discuss.

"I can't help feeling this worry that maybe, something of our connection may have helped save him if I'd only known how," Velli said.

She felt this, too, at her core.

Fira nodded again.

Tension built in the room.

Those words: *His mother blamed me entirely for his death*. They still hung in the air, heavy.

Fira took a deep breath in, and Velli waited, expecting words of soothing or some sort of perspective.

Instead, Fira pursed her lips, and blew a stream of air.

To Velli's astonishment, she could sense the texture of the air from Fira's breath. It was pink, and soft, and tinged with love at the heart of it. And also blue, pristine, and resonant with clarity around the edges.

Fira's exhale of love and clarity swept *His mother blamed me entirely for his death* straight into the bowl of the sand. In some strange way, the sensation of the fingernails gripping at Velli's wrist had been attached to that, along with the choking feeling at her neck. Both of these things lifted from Velli as though the whole thing hung together with twine.

All of it landed in the bowl of sand, which accepted them without comment.

For a moment, Velli fancied that the small bowl of sand was actually a much larger desert, self-contained within a small porcelain holder. She felt the words in the sand and the strictures of the nails and the necklace in the sand were being bathed in hot, hot sun, and baked until they started to dissolve away.

"Breathe," Fira said. "Breathe deep."

Velli breathed in, a little more deeply than she'd been able to do in some time. It was a deep, shuddering breath that seemed to come into parts of her lungs that had been clouded with grief.

She started to cry.

"Breathe," Fira repeated. "Hold the stone."

Velli caressed the stone with her thumb, letting sobs bring water down her cheeks.

"You're doing fine," Fira said. "Be with the sadness."

As Velli cried, she felt the angst of the whole situation thundering throughout her being, all of the many layers of feelings which she'd felt at various times, and suppressed at others.

Anger, pain, shame, regret, denial, frustration, grieving, loneliness, fear, hope, love.

At the bottom of it all was love.

After a long and jagged crying session, Velli looked up at Fira through moist eyes, and let out another shuddering sigh.

Fira handed her a clean, folded handkerchief, which Velli used to dry her face.

"How are you now?" Fira asked.

Velli investigated.

Her throat felt clear now, and she could breathe fully into her lungs for the first time in ages. But her shoulders still felt weighted down, and her heart felt heavy.

She reported these findings to Fira, who nodded.

"That's good progress," she said. "You can see if your heart and your shoulders ease up on their own over time, or you're always welcome to come back and see me again if you need to."

Velli smiled, triumphantly.

"Set the stone in the water," Fira said.

Velli slid it into the bowl of water, and felt all the electricity and tension which she'd felt around herself since the funeral dissolving away.

It felt amazingly freeing, but one item remained that weighed on Velli heavily.

Velli hesitated. "May I asked you one more question before I go?" she asked.

"Yes," Fira replied.

"I'm very worried about where my cousin is now," Velli admitted. "He was challenged by some things, and I am not certain whether he's crossed over well to the afterlife or not."

Fira frowned. "Pick up the gray stone," she said.

Velli did so.

She closed her eyes.

And immediately she saw him.

Deruth and Velli were sitting on a fallen tree that reached out far over the river.

They were younger—it was a few years before Velli's mother put her on the courting circuit and Velli attracted the attention of Magistrate Starring.

Velli had been crying about something. In the relationship between Velli and Deruth, they took turns being the strong one. Over the past few months, Deruth had been struggling with being bullied at the shop where he worked as an apprentice printer, and his time with Velli had been a kind relief for him.

But today Deruth reached his arm around Velli's shoulders, and held her close.

"I will always be there for you, cousin," he told her. "You can always count on me."

Velli reflected that she felt absolutely safe with him.

In the present, Velli heard Fira say, "Hold very still, and open your eyes."

Velli opened her eyes, and saw Deruth, right there!

He was standing in the room with them, looking both there and not there—but his presence was unmistakable.

His form was gray and colorless, but his eyes were very earnest.

His voice sounded watery, and he said. "I promised to always be there for you, cousin."

Velli could see a thin chain or a cord of some kind, attaching Deruth's heart to Velli's shoulders and heart.

Her own heart started to pound.

It was that feeling of being attached to an anchor which wanted to pull her over into the spirit realm.

She coughed.

Fira stood up. "Deruth, you have a good heart," she said. "But the dead and the living cannot be so tightly bound, or it will pull the living into the realm of the dead. Velli, Deruth, may I have your permission to clear this chain? Deruth, you can still help her from a distance, and Velli, you can still talk with him on the corners of the year."

Velli felt as if she was having a panicky attack. "Yes, yes, please clear it," she said.

Deruth nodded, solemnly.

Velli caught the impression he would have liked to have kept the bond, but that he was wanting to support his cousin.

Fira picked up the candle from the table and held it right in the middle of the cord. She picked up a pinch of salt and tossed it on Velli, who noticed that it smelled of herbs, and tossed another pinch through the shadowy form of Deruth.

Then Fira dipped her fingers in the bowl of water and flicked them at Velli, who winced when the cool drops of water hit her face. Fira flicked another few droplets through Deruth.

The candle burning the cord started to put up heavier smoke.

Watching, Velli was astonished to see the cord turn a shade of pink, and then an orange, and then a hot red.

She could have sworn that she smelled melting metal.

The cord started to melt and dissolve away in both directions, and Velli heard a wind pick up, and she felt as if she were standing on the edge of the great roaring desert which she had sensed in the bowl, and the water droplets on her forehead evaporated immediately.

She saw herself standing on one edge of the great span of sand, and she could sense Deruth standing at the other end of the sands.

They held out their hands toward each other.

Two friends who had been each other's comfort in a family and a city that offered them both a lot of turmoil.

Velli felt an enormous surge of love flowing to her from the distant Deruth, and she found herself sending a tremendous wave of love in return.

I will always be grateful for you, she seemed to hear his voice say. *Never forget that.*

She smiled, blinking back tears.

And it was not your fault, the voice said.

Velli leaned back.

She found herself nestling back into the rocking chair, and rocking slowly forward and back.

Fira was praying over her, saying words to bless her, naming incidents and situations in Velli's life for which she felt stress but which she definitely had not said a word to Fira about.

The room felt like a cozy world unto themselves, and Velli felt peace circling around her like a delicious blanket.

"Set the gray stone in the sand," Fira said.

Velli carefully, lovingly, set the stone in the sand, with an almost reverent attitude.

Fira nodded with satisfaction. "Now he is laid to rest," she said solidly. "Now he is finally laid to rest, after the one who loves him the most can wish him his peace."

Velli took a deep breath in, and sat up straighter and stronger than she had since the time that she'd first learned of Deruth's death.

"My heart is free," she said. "That was extraordinary. You do that kind of thing every week?"

She stared at Fira, looking for confirmation.

Fira grinned back, her olive-toned skin gleaming in the dwindling light.

They must have been working for a few hours without Velli's being aware.

"Every day," Fira said cheerfully. "Except my days off."

She squeezed Velli's shoulder happily, and Velli laughed in surprise at the lightness she felt inside her heart.

"What makes me glad today is that you look alive again," Fira said. "This was a good day's work."

Velli sat in the garden alone for a while, as the sunlight faded, and as her own thoughts settled.

She hadn't known exactly what she'd be looking for when she came to the Women's House—the women who had told her about it had been a little vague about what she might find there—but she did feel peace.

She wasn't sure whether future waves of grief would find her again, but for the moment, she was in an oasis.

And she suspected that if and when new waves of grief for her cousin came up, she'd be able to handle them better.

Placing two hands over her heart, as though absorbing the last of the light from the sun and the last of her own pause before she'd need to get up and head back to the Hub and the train and home, Velli savored the feeling: Once again, at least for the moment, she could feel peace.

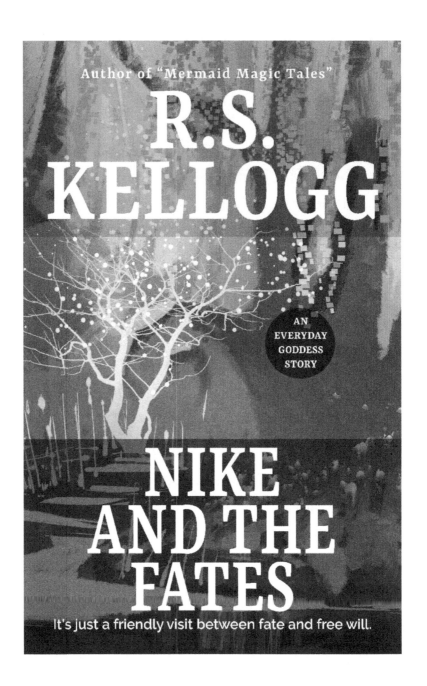

Author of "Mermaid Magic Tales"

R.S. KELLOGG

AN
EVERYDAY
GODDESS
STORY

NIKE AND THE FATES

It's just a friendly visit between fate and free will.

Nike and the Fates

by R.S. Kellogg

Nike the Goddess of Victory was on a mission.

She'd arrived at the cave of the Fates flush with determination that the Fates would hear her cause, folding her wings behind her in a tidy fashion as she prepared to enter, ready to speak her mind.

Under her arm, Nike carried a loaf of her best lemon bread, carefully wrapped in paper towels, wax paper and twine.

Since she'd baked it herself, of course it had turned out perfectly—with an ideal crumb and just the right balance between the lemon, the agave sweetener, and the pinch of gourmet salt that grounded the whole taste experience.

Letting the long hanging vines fall behind her as she stepped into the cave entrance and pushed past the delightful pink-and-gold tapestry that kept out the cold, Nike saw the light around her change from daylight to a more shadowy ambiance. Torches on the walls burned steadily, placidly one might say.

The space smelled of tangerine, divine grace, and vetiver—a scent unique to the caves of the Fates, and that always made Nike perk up because it made it feel real that she was visiting these ancient, fascinating women.

127

The solid rock beneath Nike's feet and the timeless quality of the air—air which didn't seem to move at all but also was somehow not stagnant—made this entire cave feel as if it were a place beyond time.

Which indeed in a way it was.

In the distance, a trickle of water was audible—a stream meandered through portions of these caves. Nike always felt as if the scents and sounds of the caves of the Fates made it feel as if she were visiting some kind of a primal spa.

The walls were embedded with an archeology display's worth of human sediment from across the ages—brass cups and bowls, rings by the greatest artisans, pieces of sculpture, a few random pieces of finely wrought furniture.

Nike touched the protruding edge of what looked like a fine wall-hanging. Still soft to the touch, with individual patterns still discernable where they wove into the shape of tiny figures.

Under ordinary circumstances, this kind of fine thread count would have started to decompose after being buried in a wall for a while. But Nike had visited these caves time and again throughout the centuries. And the wall hanging was still there. It was a woman's fine handiwork of her husband's epic life. The woman had long passed over the river Styx, but this piece of her craftwork remained, along with many other items from throughout Western civilization that the Fates had deemed representative of the pinnacle of humans excelling at making the most of their destiny.

Nike smiled as she saw a series of trophies in the wall. She felt a particular sort of pride in those. She'd had a hand in helping the winners of many of them to receive these cups herself. Though many of these heroes had passed on, the records of their achievements remained.

As Nike moved forward past the victory bowls of several of her favorites, and into the crafting room of the Fates, she had a bit of a strut to her step. She'd rehearsed to herself over and over again what she wanted to say, and she had front of mind the arguments for how she planned to win the Fates over.

So she was a bit non-plussed when all three of the Fates looked up as she entered their crafting space.

She faltered, food mid-stride, and stepped down awkwardly.

Chloe, straight brown hair in a practical braid, medium height, young-faced and slender, was wearing an off-white dress and holding the divine white spindle of the life threads of the gods—Nike didn't dare look too closely, as she didn't want to see if the life of a friend was being worked with.

Lach, short and solidly built, her short brown hair held back with a headband, and her pleasant round cheeks in an inquiring smile, raised an eyebrow at Nike and set aside the thread she'd been working with. Her beige dress set off the tiger's eye necklace she was wearing nicely.

And tall Atty, wearing her customary black, hair dyed black with magenta tips that she'd flipped into an up-do that made the magenta ends spill out around her head as if they were the plume feathers of some outlandish bird, her long nose angular and her look fierce, scowled at Nike. She set her scissors aside and folded her arms.

"I brought a gift!" Nike said cheerfully, brandishing the lemon bread as if it were a shield, and striding forward to set it on the lip of the crafting table furthest from the Fates.

Against the force of the grumpiness she sensed radiating off of Atty, Nike backed up a step.

It didn't do to get on the bad side of the Fates.

Even if you were the goddess of victory.

(Perhaps especially if you were the goddess of victory.)

"What do you want?" asked Chloe politely. Nike had always liked her.

"I have come to make a request," Nike said. "I want Zeus to approve my request to upgrade my symbol of a torch with a more modern flashlight. I ask for your help to let me win the next card game I have with him."

The Fates exchanged glances. Lach cleared her throat and Atty rolled her eyes clear toward the ceiling.

"If you think we control all of Zeus' card games, we need to talk," Lach said.

Nike put a fist on her hip, feeling flustered but not willing to show it. "He insisted that the winner of the card game was up to the Fates," she said. "Are you telling me the all-knowing king of the gods doesn't know what he's talking about?"

Lach tilted her head to the side. "How much power do you think we have?" she asked wryly.

Nike bit the inside of her cheek, taken aback by the question. "I guess I don't really know," she conceded. "I had assumed you have some level of oversight over things, but then there's clearly points where free will wins the day, right? And other times where I get called on for divine intervention where I clearly have a choice whether and how much to intervene. So . . ." she glanced at the Fates. None of them had shifted their facial expressions. They were all listening to her, patiently, waiting to hear what she'd have to say. "I mean, I've come down here at least a few dozen times to beseech you on behalf of one of my athletes when something's really tough, you know?" she said. "And you've never told me you can't help."

Chloe came around the table to pick up the lemon bread and retreated with it to the kitchen.

"Or maybe you just really like my baked goods and don't mind listening to me talk about my favorites in exchange for a giftie," Nike concluded archly.

Atty snorted. "Even goddesses make supplications sometimes," she said.

"Do the others come by sometimes too?" Nike asked curiously. "I've always wondered . . . like some of the love matches Aphrodite manages to hook up can seem to come out of nowhere, you know?"

"Not every goddess feels the need to consult or supplicate the Fates," Lach said steadily. "In fact, you have by far been our most frequent visitor from among the goddesses."

Nike wasn't sure whether Lach's tone was entirely encouraging, but decided to take a leap. "Does that mean I'm your favorite?" she asked.

"You're certainly the one we have the most experience with," Atty replied.

"And have granted the most wishes to?" Nike pressed on.

"Let's just say we've talked with you far more than some of the other goddesses, like Hera," Lach said.

"Oh," Nike shrugged in a dismissive way. "I suppose that will explain why she never wins at the card games of the gods."

Lach sighed. It was a heavy sound. "It's probably time we had a conversation about what we can and can't help you with," she said.

"Oh good," Nike perked up. She loved knowing rules. It was like figuring out the structure at how to win at a game. And she loved winning at games.

"Why don't you pull up a seat next to the Fireplace of the Beyond," Lach said. "I'll ask Chloe to bring you some tea. We're just about due for a break anyway."

Nike settled into a wooden chair next to a fireplace that looked far more complicated than it needed to be, stuck her feet out in front of her toward the fire, and crossed her sandalled feet at the ankles.

The chair was skillfully designed so that even a person who had wings, such as Nike, could enjoy sitting there in comfort. So lovely. She didn't imagine the Fates had guests very often, but what limited furnishings they had here were very thoughtfully designed.

She stared at the complex mix of pipes and ornate ironwork on what Lach had called the Fireplace of the Beyond, and figured that it was maybe called that because whatever mind had designed this piece was beyond her comprehension. She could make out wrought iron mythological figures all over the fireplace. A small figure of what seemed to be Tartarus was the front right leg of the fireplace, and she could see a replica of one of Zeus's lightning bolts lancing down the side and a massive black wrought-iron snake coiled around the side and tracing a path up and around a pipe leading to the back.

"Is that thing a fire hazard?" Nike asked Chloe as Chloe handed her a warm mug of honeyed tea. She took a sniff and let the aroma warm her.

"No," Chloe said. "It is a representation of the fires of the divine in the realm we serve."

That quieted Nike right down and she regarded the fireplace with a new interest, searching carefully through the symbology emblazoned on it.

Behind her she heard the Fates tidying things up, and eventually the three of them joined her. Atty remained standing—there were apparently only three chairs.

It seemed the Fates had company even less often than she'd thought.

Nike had a vague sense that perhaps it would be good manners to offer Atty her chair, but it seemed out of order as she herself was a guest. And besides, the way that Atty lounged against the side wall like that made her appear as if she really did prefer to simply stand.

"So let us talk about destiny, and free will, and fate," Lach said.

Of course it would be Lach who led the conversation, Nike reflected. She was the one who was the least ethereal of the three. Chloe in her customary white seemed cherubic, Atty with her dark black dress seemed like she took fashion and mood inspiration from the underworld, and Lach, who generally wore neutral earth tones, was the one who actually measured life.

"Tell me," Nike said, leaning back and taking a sip of the tea. She was all ears.

"It's true that there is a certain measure of destiny at play in the lives of some beings," Lach said. "You can see it in the threads we use to measure life spans. It is marks out where people start."

"So a pauper may start with a life thread of twine, while a god begins with a life ribbon of silk," Chloe said.

"But the actions that a being takes during their allotted years have great effects on both the content and the quality of the thread," Lach continued. "Someone has the ability to either elevate or degrade their thread."

Nike raised an eyebrow. "It seems to me like there's a certain limit to how much wiggle room a person could have. Take a beggar on the street, for example. You aren't telling me that they have power to raise to a silk ribbon during their lifetime."

"It would be highly unlikely to see such a huge shift over a single lifetime," Lach said sanguinely. "But it can be changed by a couple of degrees. Of greater interest to you, of course, is what happens to the contents of the thread. You come to us to ask us to magically add little flourishes here and there— a win for a race, for example, or a fortuitous political outcome. Or a favorable marriage for some of your favorites."

"You've never said no," Nike said, and looked around at the trio of unblinking Fates. "So is it that you just like my baking then?" she asked, and laughed a bit nervously.

"Of course a loaf from the oven of the goddess of victory is never to be denied," Chloe said softly.

"But I've seen it happen—more than once—that I bring you an offering, make my request, and then the requested outcome comes true," Nike said. "What's going on with that?"

The Fates exchanged a look.

"Can you grant wishes made for life threads as long as it isn't a god?" Nike asked.

Lach snorted softly. "Zeus has his own life thread, just as anyone does," she said. "He may be playing with you in suggesting that we take time out of our day to adjust the outcome of his card games."

"That or he doesn't want to be a gracious loser," Atty said.

"Why do you want to win a card game with Zeus?" Chloe asked.

Nike sat up a little straighter. "I want him to grant me a favor," she said.

"What favor?" asked Lach.

"Well, you see, my emblem has been a victory torch forever," Nike explained. "It's what people know me by, really. And I like it, and it's certainly noble to be so associated with the powerful force of fire, but the world evolves, you know? And I'd like to have more range, and a better representation across humanity."

"So you want a replacement emblem or an extension of what's already yours?" Lach asked.

"I'd like to keep the torch—and also add flashlights and beacons," Nike said. "The man who won the card game with the gods—he gave me a really wonderful flashlight. That's a symbol I can stand with in a modern era. I want to win a card game with Zeus to ask for his favor in expanding my symbology to include something new."

"And what will Zeus' favor do for you?" asked Lach.

"Well," said Nike, feeling flustered. "He's the king of the gods. So it will be added to the pantheon lexicon, and everyone who follows me will know that when they hold a flashlight that they're holding an emblem that invokes my spirit and will. It will expand my sphere of influence and presence." She caught her stride, feeling a speech building that she hadn't known was coming. "It will allow me to be present with hikers, with campers, with rescuers. With families when their power goes out. With women walking at night carrying a flashlight. I will be there. The spirit of victory will be with them. I will upbuild their spirits."

Atty set a hand on Nike's shoulder and sighed. "Her desire is good, even if a little convoluted."

Lach grinned. "Have you followed the modernity of symbolism, Nike?"

"That sounds like something from a heavy book of philosophy," said Nike.

"It's relevant to you," said Lach. "In every symbol from the past there are modern equivalents. One thing represents another—it's part of how the world works, part of how all of us work, in fact. We sisters in this cave make, measure, and snip threads that stand in as actual lifespans elsewhere. But are we actually in those people's lives? Not really."

"Or at least not very often," Atty added reflexively.

Nike noted that Lach scowled at Atty before she went on.

"It's the same way with the modernization of symbols," Lach said. "It used to be that people would ride in chariots. Now they take cars. The cars have the same symbology as the chariots. It used to be that everyone used torches. Now they use artificial lights. These also have the same symbology."

Glancing around the cave at the torches that the Fates had set up around the crafting room, Atty groaned. "Ours are mainly for show, and because we're such traditionalists," she said.

Atty went to the wall and flicked a switch which Nike hadn't noticed before—it had blended easily in with the walls filled with artifacts. The cave became flooded with the warmth of recessed lighting.

"Hey," Nike said. "It's a totally different look."

"We mainly use them on cleaning day," Atty said. "Also when we're having work done on the walls. You know how practical my sister is."

"I do," Nike said, grinning. She sipped at her nectar-flavored drink thoughtfully, and set it aside on the little table beside her.

Atty turned the overhead lights back off, and the room became, once again, the ambiance-rich craft room of the Fates with lighting to match the mood.

"So you're telling me that the flashlights are a modern symbol of the torch, and I can have them already should I claim them, and Zeus has nothing to do with that," Nike said.

"We're telling you that they're already yours," Lach said.

Nike, feeling thrilled and delighted, stood up. She hugged herself, grinning hugely. "Well, this was a lot easier than I thought it would be," she said. "I wanted help to get Zeus's buy-in but it looks like I already have what I wanted."

"Congratulations on your win," Atty said ironically. "We'll enjoy your lemon bread."

"Thank you for the conversation," Nike said, and the sisters started to walk her to the door. "But I have to ask—if by chance you did want to make it so that Zeus lost at a card game, would you have that power?"

Lach gave a smile side-grin. "That's for us to know and you to wonder," she said.

"He's been getting a bit uppity lately," Nike continued. "He could probably stand to lose."

"I believe the odds already challenge him, especially when he plays against the goddess of victory," Lach said.

Nike chuckled. "You're a diplomat, Lach," she said. "That's what you are."

"Thank you," Lach said.

"Never choose sides amongst the gods," Nike continued. "That's really smart."

"I'm glad that you agree," Lach said. "Good luck on your future card games."

As the last of the vines fell across the mouth of the cave of the Fates, hiding the entryway from all but the sharpest of eyes, Nike looked up into a light drizzle of rain.

Not the best of weather, but nothing Nike couldn't handle.

She spread her wings for the flight back to her own home and then, on an impulse, she unhooked the flashlight she'd had clipped to her belt.

She clicked it on, and aimed it in the direction she needed to go, and ascended through the gentle spring shower with a beam of her own light, blessed by herself, the goddess of victory. And also, by her friends, the Fates.

About the Author:

R.S. Kellogg writes in the fantasy Breadcove Bay series and the Agratica series, as well as exploring other story worlds and non-fiction topics.

For more information about future books and other projects, please visit www.rskellogg.com.

Sign up for the RKI newsletter to receive updates on new releases, additional content, and more! Go to rskellogg.com.

Look for these other titles by R.S. Kellogg, available at online retailers!

**Everyday Goddess Stories, Volume 1
by R.S. Kellogg**

Women and goddesses face adventures large and small in this new collection.

From the wilderness of a remote camp site to the cultivated trees of a backyard, the settings in this book introduce five unique stories of exploration and wonder.

Whether these heroines seek out their challenges or their adventures seek out them, changes are coming for all of them.

This collection features five tales of goddesses brushing the mortal realm or everyday women encountering the mystical, including:

The Empress Kuan Yin, in which Kuan's Yin's search for the balance point of the year begins in a suburban backyard.

Try Not to Get Lost in the Woods, in which Betty, hiking alone, loses her way as the sun goes down.

Artemis the Midwife, in which Bethany faces a surprise storm when she goes camping with her children.

Tia's Eclipse, in which a superstitious seeker looks for a place away from tourists to watch the coming eclipse.

Artemis and the Cats, in which Penelope chases her dog after he finds an unexpected escalator to a realm of the gods.

Buy this collection and receive all five of the above stories, gathered together for the first time in this book.

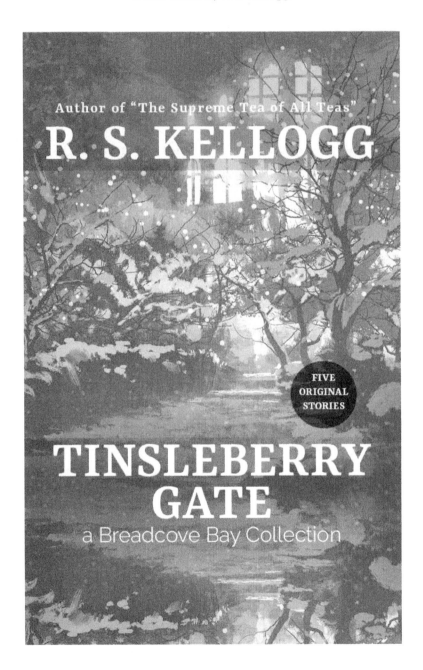

Author of "The Supreme Tea of All Teas"

R. S. KELLOGG

FIVE
ORIGINAL
STORIES

TINSLEBERRY GATE
a Breadcove Bay Collection

Tinsleberry gate works like a charm . . . until it works too well.

The Northernmost Hub Train Station protocols keep magic from making a mess.

Charms on the platform gates keep things running smoothly.

But sometimes even the best safeguards fail to keep problems at bay.

Five original fantasy stories—first published here—explore the magical portal of the Tinsleberry Gate, including:

The Medic and the Enchanted Train Station, Banning the medic works a shift during a week the Tinsleberry Gate acts up. How will he deal with what comes?

The True Tears of a Fine Romance, Jeribeth navigates the station with her fiancé on the way to their wedding and honeymoon.

The Ice Queen's Shoes, Della misses her train on a day magic lays thick around the station.

The Wishes of Norrit and Hale, the magical, legendary Norrit and Hale match wits with the station.

In Search of Debulon's Desires, Hub Boss Tamara and her team sort out problems with the Tinsleberry Gate.

Buy this collection and read all five of the above stories, published for the first time in this book.

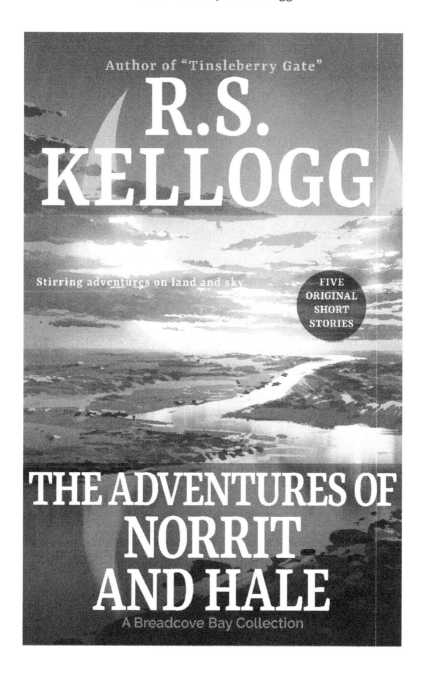

Author of "Tinsleberry Gate"

R.S. KELLOGG

Stirring adventures on land and sky.

FIVE ORIGINAL SHORT STORIES

THE ADVENTURES OF NORRIT AND HALE

A Breadcove Bay Collection

The Adventures of Norrit and Hale by R.S. Kellogg
A Breadcove Bay Collection

Join Norrit and Hale for stirring adventures on land
and across the sky.

The lives of Norrit and Hale, patron saints of grandparents, usually run predictably: gather star dust and moon dust in a big red balloon by night. Use the harvest to fuel wish-granting machinery at Starry-Eyed Station that serves requests of grandparents for their grandchildren (and sometimes requests of grandchildren for themselves).

But occasionally, surprises knock them off their typical ways of doing things . . .

This collection of five original fantasy stories—first published here—explore the magical adventures of Norrit and Hale:

Norrit and Hale: An Origin Story, reveals what happens when Hale decides to take his old friend Norrit a birthday gift on an eventful day.

In **Norrit and Hale and the Ash on the Wind,** the two old friends fly through smoky air on one of their nighttime flights. What they find in the morning surprises them.

In **Norrit and Hale and the Great Balloon Race,** the two old friends return from their night flight to find unexpected visitors at Starry-Eyed Station.

In **Norrit and Hale and the Knitting Brigade,** Norrit receives an unusual letter with a surprising request.

In **Norrit and Hale and the Dance of the Gods,** Norrit and Hale visit Tinsleberry Town for planned errands and a life-changing conversation.

Buy this collection and receive all five of these original stories.

Born of Tides: Mermaid Magic Tales, Volume 1
By R.S. Kellogg

Mermaids and magic collide in this new collection.

Land walking mermaids have the best of both worlds: They explore the depths of the seas propelled by powerful tails, and get to have fun with amusing humans when they change their tails to legs and go up onto land. And of course they love it when some of their fun is at the expense of the humans.

But sometimes, with more than fun and games and stake, mermaids need a little help from the humans . . . and sometimes, to their chagrin, they feel compelled to help these primitive land-dwellers, who are so far beneath them (evolutionary-speaking).

These six tales of merfolk adventures explore the magic of merfolk and the humans they share a fantasy planet with, including:

A Cold Mermaid Tale, the Luminator confronts a frozen cottage with an unopening door.

A Story Like Water, Maynson works as the greeter at the top of stairs coming *up* from a pool.

Water in the Dark, land walking mermaid Leora attempts to keep herself distracted with books during witching hour.

An Unexpected Mermaid, Blune follows an unusual late-night distress call out to the family barn.

Mermaid Whispers in the Dark, Nat awakens beneath a great oak near the coast to hear voices on an extra-magical night.

Midnight Mersong, the potent song of a merman calls a young woman down from her bedroom.

Also includes a bonus story—**Norrit and Hale: An Origin Story** from *The Adventures of Norrit and Hale.*

Buy this collection and receive all six of the above stories, gathered together for the first time in this book.

Sneak Peak Story Preview:
A Cold Mermaid Tale

On the following pages, please enjoy "A Cold Mermaid Tale," the first story from **Mermaid Magic Tales, Volume 1,** a collection by R.S. Kellogg available at online retailers!

Author of "Tinsleberry Gate"

R.S. KELLOGG

A BOREALIS UNIVERSITY STORY

A COLD MERMAID TALE

When the lake freezes it takes help to survive...

Story Preview:

A Cold Mermaid Tale

by R.S. Kellogg

With fingers trembling and freezing within her red gloves, even with the boost of all the heat her internal nature could provide, the Luminator struggled to get the door open on the small split-level cottage built on the rim of Sapphire Lake, a ten-minute walk from the edge of Borealis University.

A cold fog was thickening her thoughts, which currently flowed along like a muddy stream. Though she shook her head, she could not clear the thick, congested feeling.

There was something unnatural about this cold.

The scent of the freezing forest and lake smelled overly frost-bitten, as if the snow sprites had not just nibbled on the edges of reality but had actively chomped down hard, and refused to release their prey. Everything had a look and a feel tinged with grayness like frostbite, and edged in white.

Great trees standing tall around the lake postured as if they were the giants who actually owned the place, and the Luminator would have been glad to let them have it entirely. A couple of enormous pines grew close enough to the cottage that the branches—heavy with snow—nearly brushed the cottage's side.

The Luminator had reflected the first time she'd seen the place that the cottage had been nestled into an existing gap as well as possible—but there hadn't been much of a clearing there to begin with.

The builders had probably not taken any trees down to widen the gap for the cottage, which had probably been a wise move.

This part of the woods was typically especially wild and unusually awake.

Even the trees could have opinions.

But today, the usual alertness of this place had also been replaced with the same sleepy, sluggish feeling. Which was so out of the ordinary that it contributed to the sense that something here was wrong.

Despite being wedged in between trees, the side of the cottage that faced the road didn't need to be wide to begin with, as the upper-level rooms went in a straight line all the way back, and the lower level was located below the lake.

The upper half of the house suited the occupant when she chose to use legs and entertained land creatures; the lower half was for when she chose her tail.

The Luminator's breaths hung heavy on the late afternoon air: a cloud with each exhale. It was so cold the air caught in her lungs. Her black hair was tied back in a thick ponytail that left her ears exposed beneath her hat, so they were also freezing. Tiredness made her body sag with the depletion she felt whenever she faced the rare temperature below the range which she could happily tolerate. Her feet within her thick winter boots felt completely numb; her knees ached.

Her fingers were shaking harder as she futilely knocked against the door, as hard as she could, for the third time. She noticed that the noise this time was softer than the first two times she had knocked—and that her strength was fading. She felt as if she were wasting away—as if only the warmth of her heart and core kept her alive, and even that seemed to be dulling.

It was so rare for her to be frozen out like this, even in extreme cold, that it hadn't crossed her mind to consider it a possibility when she'd bundled into her warmest things, thrown a couple of items into her robe's pockets that may come in handy, and hurried out to check on the cottage.

If she'd realized it would be this cold before she'd left her workroom, she may never have come. Usually even the coldest days around Breadcove Bay gave the Luminator little trouble—she was, after all, a being birthed from fire. But today, on the fourth day of a terrible cold snap, the Luminator struggled to grapple with even such simple a matter as the frozen door. She couldn't feel her hands. Her face felt like a frozen mask, and she could feel a cough coming on from deep inside her lungs.

Not good.

Not good.

She sensed downward into the ground for the great heat below the surface, seeking to call up reserves of warmth to support her, but something below the ground here was slippery like oil and disorienting. She pulled her consciousness right back up into herself as soon as she realized that whatever barrier was there wouldn't let her through.

There was no additional heat to be had.

So there wasn't much time.

If fuel of her internal flame were to start sputtering—if it risked going out—the Luminator could be looking at the end of herself.

Even in her cold, muddy thinking, she had enough of a sense of self-preservation to be careful. She could spare perhaps two minutes more at the door, and then if she failed to open it, she must turn back for her own sake, and pray that she could make it back to her workroom in time, and that the cottage occupant would survive somehow on her own.

The front of the cottage smelled like icy wind. There was no wood smoke, and no sign that the cottage was currently inhabited. It was so blastedly cold, even for Breadcove Bay, that the Luminator suspected interfering magic.

Against the dull thud of her own heartbeat, the Luminator thought that hopefully, hopefully, the occupant of the house had decided to choose the lower half of the house and port away before the current cold snap had descended to its worst.

—This despite the fact that the rest of the university staff hadn't seen the teacher who lived in the cottage for three days, and despite the fact that the Luminator's own inner spark, which she trusted beyond everything else as a guide, had screamed to her that she must do something when Shanning—another fellow teacher—had stopped by a half-hour earlier to mention the teacher's absence.

They'd looked at each other, and Shanning had half-heartedly offered to come, but they both knew he wouldn't survive this kind of cold as a human.

It had been egotistical of her not to consider whether it might be too cold for her as well, really.

The fastening of the cottage door still wouldn't budge, frozen stiff.

She dropped her hands away from the door, helpless, head drooping. Then, the memory nudged her of the handful of small items which she'd shoved in her pocket before she'd left. Perhaps one of them may be useful.

Digging through the large side-pocket of her robe with clumsy fingers, she pulled out a length of red twine.

It there was an element of interfering magic to the deep cold of the day, perhaps this might help.

As quickly as she could manage with her stiffening hands, but still carefully, the Luminator wrapped an end of the red twine around the latch.

Then she breathed a fire word aloud: an unbinding.

As if it had been a knife slipping across warm butter, the door eased open, creaking mightily and leaving water sliding down the door and dripping into a puddle across the floor as it went.

Thank the sun.

The Luminator threw herself into the cottage with a burst of energy fueled by rising fear—she must find out if the cottage was empty, and she must find heat—and she slammed the door shut.

Her ears pricked at a deep crackling sound as the edges of the door immediately froze shut again.

Shivering heavily, the Luminator realized she'd just committed herself to staying in the cottage until the end of the cold snap, probably: she couldn't expect to unseal the door again and make it across the distance over to the campus and keep her remaining warmth.

The trouble was that the interior of the cottage seemed to be just as cold as the outside, if not colder.

Frost covered the walls of the little front room, and the fireplace had what looked like a foot of snow in it.

How had that even filled up? Shouldn't there be a way to block it at the top?

The Luminator wrapped her arms around herself to retain more heat and moved quickly across the blue rag quilts on the weathered boards of the front room floor and through the gap in the floral curtains that divided the first room from the next room beyond.

The second room was a kitchen. Everything tidily arranged, with pots hanging in a neat line on the wall, and dishes stacked on a shelf. The table was clear except for an unlit lamp and a tidy stack of books next to a tidy stack of student papers. The dishes in the sink had clearly been abandoned before they were cleaned—with food still frozen in place on the plates. Looked like the remains of fish and potatoes for two.

Which meant someone had been a guest in the house for the most recent meal.

The Luminator shook her head. With everything in the house so chilled, it would be difficult to track how old the food on the dishes might be.

She wrapped her scarf around her neck a little more snugly, and moved through the far doorway of the kitchen, aware that there were two more rooms above water—two more places that she could check.

If her friend wasn't in either of those two spaces, the Luminator would return to the kitchen to see what warmth magic she could conjure to keep herself alive until the cold snap fell.

The next room was the bedroom, with a full cozy-but-empty bed, and a closet filled with a few teacher's robes and some simple dresses. Only two pairs of shoes on the floor. All very tidy, the bed cleanly made.

Impatient now, the Luminator crossed this room quickly, sparing only a glance to either side of the tidy bed to be sure that nobody had fallen and frozen on the floor in here.

Finally, she reached the last curtained door, which would lead her into the last room.

The last room was a strange room for a strange house—a combined bathroom and powder room, with a toilet, an enormous ornate tub, and a dressing table; yet also a transition room, with stairs that led down into the lake side of the house, which as near as the Luminator had heard from the descriptions was actually something more along the lines of a cave.

The Luminator pushed through the curtain into the last room, planning to do a quick check before she'd retreat into the kitchen, where she'd planned to start up the stove and get herself, at last, warm.

But as soon as she arrived in the room, and the shock of even-colder air in the space, she stopped, heart pounding.

It was an eerie space, with strange light. The room was lit only by the high windows, and by the luminous seashells that Maryssa had mounted to the walls of entrance that went into the frozen lake, giving the coloring of the room a strange green cast to it.

Maryssa the mermaid lay unconscious in the tub, her face pale with a cast of blue, her head tilted back at an angle. The water of the tub was frozen. The flippers of her great tail extended out of the tub like a sculpture, with a thick sheen of ice coating every inch of her great blue fins and the scales of her tail. Her face looked contorted in pain, eyes clenched shut, nose wrinkled. Her fingers were in a frozen grip on the edges of the porcelain tub.

"Oh Maryssa," breathed the Luminator, and instantly regretted opening her mouth as now her tongue and throat felt cold—this room was noticeably colder than the rest of the house. Probably because the watery entrance to the lake side of the house was frozen solid and emanating a heavy chill.

It was like being in an ice house.

She felt her inner spark dim even more.

The Luminator took an instinctive step backward, toward warmth, obviously she'd gotten here too late and she must hole up in the kitchen until things warmed up outside.

Her foot crunched against a patch of snow that she hadn't noticed.

A faint cracking sound in the tub drew her attention.

And Maryssa's eyes opened.

The look she gave the Illuminator was shocked and dazed.

The Luminator nodded at her, as if to say, "Oh, good. You're alive!" But she didn't dare to open her mouth again in the frozen room. Instead, she retreated backwards, quickly, feeling her inner spark growing wispy and faint. Back through the cozy bedroom, back to the kitchen. She tied her twine around the controls of the stovetop, and dumped a tiny spark of her own flame to serve as a pilot light.

The stovetop roared to life.

Fire.

Finally, fire.

Her native element.

The Luminator peeled the gloves back from her hands, leaned forward, and stuck her hands *into* the fire, plunging them deep into the flames.

Ah.

That felt better.

The rest of her body shuddered in a massive shiver as she realized exactly how cold the rest of her had gotten.

The cold at her core was tenacious. She had to shake her shoulders and stomp her feet to get it to start to break its hold.

She let the fire soak into her skin.

The part of herself that was a little bit human stepped aside.

And the part of herself that was a flame elemental drank in revitalization. She felt the fire caress her like a concerned lover, soaking deeply into the bones of her hands, filling her blood with a life-giving spark that began to course through her system, bringing fresh new vitality up through her arms, and to her great heart, which lit up like a torch being refueled, and poured fresh new heat into her secondary fire below—her soul spark.

The heat flooded out through her body—through her chest, her waist, her back, down through her legs and up through her neck and her heat.

It wasn't an easy fix or a fast one. She had to stay there for several minutes, allowing the heat to course through her, letting her awareness come back.

A fog that had thickened her thoughts seemed to be burning itself off, freeing her mind to move more nimbly now, sharpening her perception and perspective.

Her eyesight refined, and now she could see the subtle colors of the flame—how it was a blue around the base, and had a hollow darkish bottom, and grew into a bright yellowy-orangey effervescence at its top.

She felt the warmth from flame sink into her bones, allowed it to go down into the very marrow, where it sank into her essence and burned out the tiredness she'd felt, the lethargy.

The flames at her heart and at her core expanded, began to burn taller again, and then flooded outward, filling her whole being with light and exultation.

She breathed in a breath that warmed itself up immediately upon entering her nostrils. The air hit the heat at her core and woke her inner flames to even higher levels of happy dancing, and the weight of her stress and worry over survival melted clean away from her skin. Any whisper of a cough evaporated from her lungs, and she could feel them healthy and happy with every breath she drew. Every inch of her felt bathed in light.

It felt as if even her gaze was filled with light, and as if anything that she looked at seemed to be a bit brighter and more vibrant. Sweat rose from her armpits and between and under her breasts, and she realized that her human side had received about enough of the flame.

She could have excused her human side for a moment, stepped right into the fire realm and warmed herself up completely, but now was not the right time.

She needed to have secure space for that kind of thing. And the cold was a cold that she didn't trust. This space was one that was not her own.

And Maryssa, alone in the other room, needed assistance which the Luminator was strong enough now to render.

How best to free Maryssa from the tub?

The Luminator cocked her head to the side. She'd need to thaw the water, obviously, to get Maryssa free. But how best to do that in the frozen room?

She couldn't very well haul the tub filled with ice and Maryssa back into the kitchen, so she'd need to bring the warmth out there herself.

The lamp seemed like a good probable object. The Luminator scooped it from the table, removed the hurricane shield, lit the tiny flame, and replaced the cover. Then she carefully carried it from the kitchen, leaving the stove top burning merrily with happy tiny fire sounds as she went.

Lifting the curtain carefully to first the bedroom and then the bathroom, the Luminator brought the lamp to Maryssa, whose eyes were still open, but drooping.

The cheerful radiance from the lamp lit the space with fresh life, making everything look slightly better in the space— or as better as things could be when someone is still clearly freezing to death in a tub.

"I've come to help you," the Luminator said cheerfully, then closed her mouth hard as the cold air that had entered her mouth between words chilled so fast that she could feel the roots of her teeth.

Kneeling on the freezing tile floor to get the lamp settled next to the tub, the Luminator reflected that she could draw the fire up from the lamp and use it to heat the outside of the tub— gradually freeing Maryssa.

A good plan, but it failed.

As soon as the Luminator had settled in place and got the lamp where she wanted it, the tiny flame, which had started to fade from the moment it had come into the bathroom, went out entirely.

The room was once again lit only by the high windows, and by the luminous seashells that Maryssa had mounted to the walls of entrance that went into the frozen lake.

It felt like a crypt in the room with the sudden snuffing of the light.

Now that the Luminator was closer to Maryssa, she saw that the middle-aged mermaid was wearing what appeared to be a coat made of luminous sea stars, which glowed faintly as well.

She wanted to say that she hoped that the coat was keeping Maryssa warm, but the suffering look on Maryssa's face and the freeze that was rapidly settling into the Luminator's skin, once again dulling her inner spark, told her now was not the time for gentle humor—a judgment call she felt a trifle smug about being able to follow, despite the effect the chill had on muddying her thoughts.

"Be right back," she said, as quickly as possible so as to let very little chilled air into her mouth.

She could have sworn that the mermaid gave a ghost of a nod.

Retreating to the kitchen, the Luminator felt a flash of irritation to see that the stovetop had gone out.

"I leave you alone for two minutes and you can't handle being on your own?" she asked it.

She set the lamp back down on the table, and inspected the stove. The simple knot she'd tied with the red twine had turned to ask and hung together with a sheen of ice around it.

Shaking her head at the obnoxious kitchen, the Illuminator fished in her pocket for fresh red twine—there was alarmingly little left—and she got enough so that she could make a new tidy knot on the controls of the stovetop.

Once again, she dropped a bit of her own essence into the stove in place of the evaporated pilot light, and once again the stovetop sprang into life.

Hunting around for something more substantive than a lamp, the Luminator's attention was caught by the kitchen broom.

It would do.

She prepped the passageway and lessened the fire hazard by shoving wide open the curtains to first the bedroom and then also the bathroom.

The freezing air that rushed through from the bathroom to the bedroom to the kitchen which followed her as she returned sent shivers all the way down her back and made her feel as if she were being breathed at by a frost giant.

But the light on the stove had held steady—it was still going.

The Luminator picked up the broom and lit the end of the straw with the flame, then carried it like a torch over to the tub and frozen Maryssa. She slid the burning broom underneath the tub, watching as the fire began to burn along the shaft, and then realizing with horror that there was nothing in the bathroom she could see which would serve as fuel to the flame.

An idea seized her—perhaps her thoughts were not quite so hampered by this dogged muddy feeling as to slow her entirely—and she raced back to the kitchen, slipping against a small patch of ice she hadn't noticed before in the bedroom and catching herself on the doorframe to the kitchen, then scooping up the stack of student papers and bolting back to the fire underneath the tub.

It was far more important to save the life of a teacher than to grade those papers, in her book.

But as she reached the bathroom, she saw that the end of the broom was smoldering—and despite her best effort she couldn't revive it. The flame had once again gone out.

Maryssa looked at the papers, and then at the Illuminator, with an expression that looked even more pained than usual.

"I know, I know," said the Illuminator. "I'm sorry I'm the only one that could come and help you. I know that you and I haven't gotten along always too well, but I'm going to have to see what I can do here, because nobody else can survive this cold. I don't know how to get you warmer, though."

Maryssa's eyes darted to the right a few times.

The Illuminator scowled, following the direction of Maryssa's gaze, and her sight landed on a water heater in the corner.

She moved over to it, taking a careful look at what was there.

Hard black surface, oil canister nearby on the floor.

Oil canister.

The Luminator smiled. She could work with this.

She picked up the canister of oil.

Half-full.

She frowned, and did some mental fire magic math, her favorite type of both calculus and spells, and arrived at a decision.

"Bear with me here and don't be scared," the Luminator said to Maryssa. "It'll be two seconds."

She'd determined that the worst of the cold was definitely coming from the lake. The Luminator reached into her pocket for a small magic hand-mirror, which she propped against the water heater, aiming it back toward the lake. The water on the lake got, if anything, colder, but the cold from the room began to clear.

"That's more like it," the Luminator said. "I think we have a patch of safety."

What happened next, Maryssa would have been hard pressed to explain to anybody, but she rarely tried. When asked later how exactly the Luminator had saved her from the Great Cold Snap during the Winter War of the Ice Queen, Maryssa would just press her lips together and raise her eyebrows.

"Magic," was typically her complete reply.

And if the listener knew the Luminator at all, they'd merely nod knowingly even if they didn't fully understand. After all, the Luminator was one of the most magical and mysterious teachers at the university.

If the listeners didn't know the Luminator quite as well, and they tried to ask further questions, "She brought fire to the ice," was the complete answer they'd get.

And this was satisfactory for nearly all of them.

But what actually happened in that little room was a bit more complex.

Judging by the look on Maryssa's face, the Luminator thought that if she hadn't already been nearly frozen to death she may have fainted with fear.

Because she had her eyes open with the Luminator *stepped aside from her human part* for just a minute at left that standing there smiling at Maryssa reassuringly while the Luminator's fire side drank the oil and pushed from her hands a controlled inferno of intense heat that melted the water in the tub—first the tub warmed, then the water near the edges started to melt as the water dripped from Maryssa's tail, and then the Luminator lessened the intensity of the heat a bit as the heat continued to radiate through, making water from ice, and gradually thawing the mermaid in the tub along with it.

The room smelled of scorched sea stars, and singed hair.

Maryssa finally waved weakly at the fiery half of the Illuminator, which was still sending an inferno of flame at the tub.

"You good?" asked the Illuminator in her fire voice.

Maryssa winced and nodded, and the Illuminator laughed and dropped her fiery temperature by several degrees, and stepped back into her human side.

Shaking herself and running her hand down her own slightly singed human ponytail, the Illuminator came over to Maryssa, digging through her pocket once again as she did so.

"I can't believe you made it in through the cold," croaked Maryssa, in a voice that sounded as if it were still thawing.

"Me either," the Illuminator said.

The hair on Maryssa's head looked as if it had far more white strands than when the Illuminator had last seen her. And the wrinkles around her eyes looked deeper, her face more drawn. She looked as if she'd need a week to rest after her ordeal.

Probably worst of all, Maryssa's tail smelled faintly of baking fish. The Illuminator pulled an enormous jar of Mermaid Salve out of her pocket.

"I didn't know if this would come in handy, but it looks like you could use it," she said.

Maryssa nodded.

The Illuminator opened the jar and worked Mermaid Salve all along Maryssa's tail.

The temperature in the room was nice and warm, now that the ice had thawed. The magic mirror was doing a remarkable job of keeping the cold from the frozen lake back.

"Why didn't you set up the magic mirror first?" asked Maryssa.

The Illuminator shook her head. "Brain was foggy," she said. "I could barely think to stay alive. How did you come to be in the tub?"

Maryssa sounded peeved. "I was trying to go into a hibernation state," she said. "I can survive much lower temperatures that way. I mostly made it before the worst of the cold came."

"I'm glad you survived," the Illuminator said.

"Really?" Maryssa said.

The two of them weren't the best of friends.

"I'd hate to be the one who had to teach the students about water magic," the Illuminator retorted.

Maryssa snorted. "Well I'm glad you got to be a hero today," she said.

The Illuminator grunted with what sounded like agreement, and continued to work the salve deep into the grooves of Maryssa's long tail. "I'll have to leave the rest of the jar for you when I go, so you can take care of it on your own. It might be sensitive for a while."

Maryssa yawned. "I'll just turn into my human form," she said. "I feel as if I could sleep for a week. But you can leave the jar. I'll definitely be using it eventually."

The Illuminator grinned. "Deal," she said. "I'll even bring you another broom."

"Oh, you'd better be bringing me another broom," Maryssa said. "I can't believe you turned mine into a torch like that."

The Illuminator chuckled. "Just had to work with what I had on hand," she said.

"And the papers are probably ruined." Maryssa said contemplatively.

The papers, which had gotten dropped across the floor in the excitement, were now all completely burned to ash.

"Well, it wasn't like it was the class final," the Illuminator replied.

Maryssa's breath had steadily deepened, and was now fully back to normal. "I suppose I should thank you," she said.

"No problem," the Illuminator said. "I'm sure you'd do the same for someone else."

There was an interesting texture to the moment that followed, as if Maryssa was thinking over whether she *would* do the same for someone else and concluding that she very likely would not.

"Anyway," the Illuminator said, "Once things warm up a bit outside, I'll go back and tell the staff that you're fine but that Shanning will need to cover your classes for the rest of the week while you rest up."

"Oh, thank you," Maryssa said smugly. "Yes, let's make Shanning do it."

Shanning, who was able to guess that Maryssa might be in trouble but hadn't been able to save her himself.

Shanning, the eager newest faculty member still wanting to prove himself.

Shanning, who could handle any of the main bodies of magic, and was native to none of them while knowledgeable of all.

Yes, they both nodded. Shanning would do nicely to be the substitute, indeed.

To read the rest of the stories in Mermaid Magic Tales, Volume 1, by R.S. Kellogg, purchase the complete collection, now available at online retailers.

Made in the USA
Coppell, TX
14 October 2021